ALSO BY AMY HEMPEL

REASONS TO LIVE

AT THE GATES OF THE ANIMAL KINGDOM

TUMBLE HOME

A NOVELLA
AND SHORT STORIES

AMY HEMPEL

SCRIBNER

SCRIBNER
1230 Avenue of the Americas
New York, NY 10020

SCRIBNER and design are trademarks of Simon & Schuster Inc.

DESIGN BY ERICH HOBBING

Set in Garamond No. 3

Manufactured in the United States of America

1   3   5   7   9   10   8   6   4   2

Library of Congress Cataloging-in-Publication Data is available.

ISBN 0-684-83375-1

"Weekend" appeared first in *Harper's;* "Sportsman" appeared first in *GQ;* "The Annex" in
The Yale Review; "The New Lodger" in *The Quarterly;* "Church Cancels Cow" in *The Alaska
Quarterly Review;* "Housewife" in *Micro Fiction.* Parts of "Tumble Home" appeared first in
Epoch, Elle, and *Salmagundi.*

105764

For my brothers,
GARDINER and PETER

Acknowledgments

For various kinds of generosity in respect of this book, I want to thank Deborah Berke, Christine Burgin, Bernard Cooper, Liz Darhansoff, Martha Gallahue, Nan Graham, A. M. Homes, R. S. Jones, Sheila Kohler, David Leavitt, Robert Polito, Hannah Siegel, Amy Tan, Anne Kaiser Taylor, Lily Tuck, Kathryn Walker, William Wegman, and the Corporation of Yaddo.

I am especially grateful for the crucial parts played by Mark Richard, Pearson Marx, Jill Ciment, Jim Shepard, Benjamin Taylor, and, of course, Pete Dandridge.

CONTENTS

TUMBLE
HOME

Weekend

The game was called on account of dogs—Hunter in the infield, Tucker in the infield, Bosco and Boone at first base. First-grader Donald sat down on second base, and Kirsten grabbed her brother's arm and wouldn't let him leave third to make his first run.

"Unfair!" her brother screamed, and the dogs, roving umpires, ran to third.

"Good power!" their uncle yelled, when Joy, in a leg cast, swung the bat and missed. "Now put some wood to it."

And when she did, Joy's designated runner, Cousin Zeke, ran to first, the ice cubes in his gin and tonic clacking like dog tags in the glass.

And when Kelly broke free from Kirsten and this time came in to make the run, members of the Kelly team made Tucker in the infield dance on his hind legs.

"It's not who wins—" their coach began, and was shouted down by one of the boys, "There's *first* and there's *forget it.*"

Then Hunter retrieved a foul ball and carried it off in the direction of the river.

The other dogs followed—barking, mutinous.

Dinner was a simple picnic on the porch, paper plates in laps, the only conversation a debate as to which was the better grip for throwing shoes.

After dinner, the horseshoes were handed out, the post pounded in, the rules reviewed with a new rule added due to falling-down shorts. The new rule: Have attire.

The women smoked on the porch, the smoke repelling mosquitoes, and the men and children played on even after dusk when it got so dark that a candle was rigged to balance on top of the post, and was knocked off and blown out by every single almost-ringer.

Then the children went to bed, or at least went upstairs, and the men joined the women for a cigarette on the porch, absently picking ticks engorged like grapes off the sleeping dogs. And when the men kissed the women good night, and their weekend whiskers scratched the women's cheeks, the women did not think *shave,* they thought: *stay.*

Church
Cancels Cow

Pheasant feathers in a plastic jack-o'lantern—this is the way people decorate graves in October across from my house. In winter they tie wreaths to the stones like evergreen pendants in December. The halved-apple faces of owls on a branch will spook you, walking at dusk as I do with my dog who finds the one real pumpkin, small on a stem, and carries it off and flings it and retrieves, leaving on the pumpkin the marks of her teeth, the only desecration in these rows of tended plots.

Or not, according to the woman at the wheel of the red Honda Civic that appears from behind the Japanese maple and proceeds past the hedge of arborvitae where she slows and then rolls down her window to say, "You should keep that dog on a leash." She says, "That dog left faces on my mother's grave."

When I realize she means feces, I say my dog didn't do it. She says yes, my dog did it. I say, "Did you *see* this dog leave feces on the grave?" She says, "I found faces on my mother's grave. I had to clean them off." I say there are other dogs that walk here. I say my dog goes in the woods before the place where the headstones start.

I leave her talking to me from her car. I walk away with my dog in the direction of my house, and she follows in her car so I turn back around and lead her through the cemetery and sit down on a random grave and take a wire brush from the pocket of my coat and begin to groom my dog, brushing slowly from the ends up to the skin so as not to tug and hurt her. I stay where I am until the woman drives away, and I stay until she reappears. When she leaves the second time, she leaves rubber in the road.

For days I see her car across the street, parked on the little-used access road, her at the wheel just watching my house where my dog patrols the yard, unmistakeable dog. I write down her license plate number, so what. I pull weeds with my back to her. And after thoughts of worse things than bricks coming flying through the windows of my house, I pull off grass-stained gloves and cross to her car and say, "You know, I'm on your side about this. *I* have relatives buried here, and I don't want to find faces on their graves."

She says, "*You* have relatives buried here?"

For peace of mind I will lie about any thing at any time.

In fact, she says, she has counted three dogs the other day from her car. Like counting cows, in the game I played in cars when the family went out on long drives.

My brother and I were told to count cows in the fields we passed along the way, me counting cows on one side of the road, my brother counting cows on the other. But if we passed a church, the person on whose side the church appeared had to start their count over again.

Why did church cancel cow? The question was not a question back then, and when I try to think why, the best I can guess is—because we were having fun? Until I mention it to my brother who says, "Don't you remember? You don't remember. It was cemetery, not church, that cancels cow."

And why it comes to me now.

The Children's Party

"Bye-bye," the baby said, his voice a little bell. "Bye-bye," he waved, as we arrived for the party at the lake.

We were stiff after driving from our house hours south in a town overrun by tourists. We put gifts on a table in the hall. The three children all had birthdays the same week.

The baby's father showed us to the porch. He poured us drinks, said, *"This*'ll change your handwriting."

The others were friends from across the lake who came up for a month every summer, tying their bull's-eye or turnabout to a cleat and hopping out onto a dock.

Between the back porch and the lake was a well-kept lawn with a grill, coals just lit, and a large decorated paper-bag piñata strung up in a shimmering willow. The baby's mother and a woman I didn't know called me over to join them beside the piñata. The woman I didn't know asked if I had a match. I didn't see the cigarette she held, and thought she meant to light the piñata. I told her, and we all doubled over picturing melting gummy bears dripping like hot wax onto the outstretched hands of the blindfolded children beneath it.

"Some little boy's scrotum get nailed to a tree?" asked one of the children's fathers from the porch. "I see three women laughing like this —" he bent over, knees pressed together, and held his crotch — "I look for a scrotum nailed to a tree."

Farther out, naked children pushed each other off a dock into the bracing lake. At the far end of the dock was a small child's slide poised above deep water. "I just put it there to scare his mother," said the baby's father, chuckling diabolically: "Look — he can go in by himself!"

Tony Peebles — handsome, hearty next-door neighbor —still had not arrived.

"Heart attack," someone said.

"Car wreck," someone else said.

"Heart attack then car wreck," came a chorus.

"Talking to someone at the store," said his wife. "He went there an hour ago. I was telling Judy, he goes to pick up the steaks, there could be a stuffed effigy of the butcher behind the counter, Tony'd engage it in conversation."

Only a couple of us knew what was taking so long. The children's dog had been killed the month before. The children felt it would be unfair to get another dog— unfair to their *former* dog. The children were in pain, and I felt I knew what to say. I said to their father, quoting a lovely poem, "Tell them this: 'The need for the new love *is* faithfulness to the old.'"

He said, "That's what I used to tell myself when I cheated on my ex-wife."

But he had agreed, and the men were picking up the children's new dog, a pup from a nearby camp.

"I hope none of you are allergic," said the baby's mother, moving aside a vase of wildflowers to make room for a cake on a plate. "It's an allergy-fest out there.

"This cake, by the way, is real chocolate," she assured us. "I'm sick of trying to force carob on you, and all of you spitting it out behind my back." Yet we saw that our health-conscious hostess was still serving the dreaded organic fig bars from the health food store in town. "Colon blasters," we called them. The baby's father had said that Colin Blaster sounded like the name of an English soccer coach.

"Tony's not back yet?" one of his friends asked.

"And he made Bruce go with him," Bruce's wife said. "Tony probably told him there was something in town he had to show him, and he took Bruce to town and the thing he had to show him was a stop sign."

We ate deviled eggs while we waited for Tony and Bruce to return with the steaks. On the drive up, I told a friend, we'd seen blueberries wild by the side of the road and birch bark peeling from the trunks of trees with towering crowns, but so far we'd seen no moose.

"If you come out with us in the canoe tomorrow, you'll see plenty of moose," she said. She described the stretch of river we would travel and the numbers of moose we would see. "But no males with antlers. They're shy. You have to wait. You see them come out to look for females in the fall."

The children called for us to watch them play with eggs. It was the game wherein you toss a raw egg gently to your partner a few feet away. Your partner tosses it back, and you widen the gap between you. The toss and retreat is repeated until all but one of the pairs has broken their eggs.

We watched, sipping drinks, until the baby's father called, "Eyes right!" and appeared in the yard to the right of the house carrying a baseball bat. The children screamed with laughter as they took turns pitching raw eggs.

"Jackpot!" they screamed, as the baby's father connected, splattering them all, including the neighbor's dog who had stopped by to cruise the grill.

Mr. Howell, emboldened by the display, retrieved from his car a sack of sheathed hunting knives. But other of the parents blew the whistle on this — high-stakes pin-the-tail-on-the-donkey not the same as batting eggs — and we strained to hear his gnarly utterances as he returned the knives to his car.

"Deadlines," one of the birthday girls announced, excusing herself from the games. "I have deadlines," she said soberly, inexplicably adjusting a gorilla mask over her face.

On the porch, in a high chair, the baby sent a bowl of Cheerios sailing off the tray.

"Dinner is shoved," said his mother, kneeling to wipe up the mess. She returned from the kitchen with a jar of baby food and a clean spoon. "What's he eating now?" asked the baby's father. He picked up the jar and mimed alarm as he "read" the label: "Deadly poison?!" This made the children spit potato salad till their parents said get a grip.

Down on the dock, a brother and sister began yelling at each other until the girl ran to their mother crying, "Dan hit me back!"

"Dan has a temper. He takes after me," said their little brother sagely.

"You mean *you* take after *him*," said their mother. "He was here first."

The baby's mother picked up a small inflated raft in the shape of a giraffe. She pointed the long spotted neck at her husband and winked at him through the two small holes in the seat. "Imagine being able to fit your legs through these," she said.

"I thought they were for your breasts," her husband said.

Bruce's wife shushed him. We heard the distant, slightly hysterical cry of a loon on the lake.

"People think they're related to ducks," said a local for our benefit, "but they're really much closer to penguins."

"You go in the lake," said Mr. Howell, "watch out for leeches. *Giant* leeches. I had to nudge a moose this morning with my boat — he was eating the lily pads I planted, and he didn't move when I yelled at him to stop. When you ram a moose from behind, you got to be prepared for more than contact. He had a row of leeches on his butt swung like fringe."

"You see the fox last night?" a neighbor asked.

"I seen a fox grab a leech off a moose's butt —" said Mr. Howell before we could shut him up.

In the absence of Tony and Bruce and the steaks, we refilled our glasses and shared the children's hot dogs. I heard the baby laughing from inside the house, and followed the sound to where he was having his bath. His mother made an ice cream cone of suds and pretended to lick it. "Aaaagh!" she said, and the baby laughed again. I knelt beside the tub and scooped up a handful of suds. I brought it to my mouth and licked. "Aaaagh!" I sputtered to the baby's delight, squinching my face in dismay.

From outside, someone called us down to see. In the road, beneath a street light, was the young moose the children had named Moosifer. As we watched, the moose went down on its front legs, kneeling in the road like a camel, its tongue slowly rolling across the spot where, earlier, a clump of crows had pecked at the soft parts under the crushed shell of a box turtle someone hadn't stopped for.

"It's Moosifer," one of the children whispered to another.

Moosifer was a female, said our moose-butt expert. You could tell by the absence of antlers.

The Children's Party

"Eyes right!" the urgent whisper of our host.

We looked to the woods where something large was making its way through the trees toward the road.

In the moment before Tony and Bruce drove up — the children's new dog barking in the car — locals and guests, we held our breath as branches broke, the magnificent rack an emblem of need that could not wait another day.

Sportsman

By rights, Jack should have headed west when his wife, Alex, left him, but they lived in California so he drove east, folding down the visor each morning against the sun. He didn't wait to find a cheap motel at night, just pulled off the road and slept cramped in the car a few hours. At dawn he thrust a stick of Right Guard up under his shirt—the rock 'n' roll shower—and drove until he found coffee. He thought that traveling alone was like being in therapy—the things you found out about yourself.

Speeding across the Bonneville Salt Flats, Jack played car golf, weaving in and out of the lanes trying to roll the Ping-Pong ball in the passenger seat well into the Styrofoam coffee cup that was on its side after spilling out most of the coffee. Jack was good at this.

Not that he'd been invited, but he was, he realized, going to New York, to the home of his friend the doctor,the closest thing to rehab he could find.

Jack signaled and changed lanes at the exit for the Long Island Expressway, and remembered Alex's directions, the way she would say "then turn left six blocks before the liquor store." He'd phoned from the last gas station. The doctor said they would be glad to see him. Jack had to ask, "Does Vicki still talk about feelings all the time?"

Vicki had given him a diary one Christmas, a blank book that stayed blank, and which Jack had titled "Jackie's Log of Feelings." Vicki was a good mimic and did a dead-on imitation of Jack as if he were a psychiatrist wincing at a patient's confession, ordering a depressed person to "just snap out of it" or leaning forward in his therapist's chair saying, simply, "Handle it."

Jack had offered to take them out to dinner, but the doctor wanted to barbecue, so Jack stopped at a market and bought three big steaks on the way. It was too soon for even Vicki to try to fix him up is what he told himself when he considered buying four.

In summer, the town was a beach resort. In realtor parlance, Vicki and the doctor lived on the wrong side of the highway, but it was still only a five-minute drive to the water.

At the door, Vicki gave Jack a kiss and a bath towel, and pointed him down the hall, which made a thick gold bracelet slide the length of her forearm to her wrist. "It's one of those 'Honey, I'm sorry' gifts," she said, and Jack said, "Nice. Get him angry again."

The doctor had a cold beer for him when Jack came out of the shower smelling of mandarin orange-scented soap. They showed him around the house, an Arts and Crafts cottage built in 1932. Since his last visit, they'd replaced the previous owner's insane wallpaper (shelves of books behind chicken wire) and pried off the bedroom floors' linoleum, the pattern of which was a photograph of carpeting, revealing wide planks of clean pine.

"We put up a detached garage," the doctor said, adding, for the nth time, "it doesn't care if you park in it or not." The tour concluded on the redwood deck the doctor had built himself.

"Things are looking pretty swep'-up around here," Jack said.

Vicki, in faded cutoffs, kicked off espadrilles and took the red butterfly chair. She observed that Jack always said he was on his way out when he called. "It's like you can't make an entrance until you've established your exit."

Jack hated for people to analyze his behavior. He hated for them to notice it. He moved to give the doctor a hand with the steaks and managed to fork one off the grill and into the coals. "Oops," he said, fishing for it. "Mine."

"Doctors can't say 'Oops,' " the doctor said. "Doctors say '*There.*' "

Jack had resisted the temptation to run his latest symptoms by the doctor, but when the doctor asked him how he was, Jack told the truth about the shoulder that had betrayed him. The doctor was in orthopedics and so gifted at treating sports injuries that he had become a team physician, retained to see to football stars. It looked glamorous to Jack—his friend going out onto the field and examining the swelling million-dollar knees. But it was really "like veterinary medicine," the doctor had told him. "You can't get a history from those guys."

"I'll give you a shot of cortisone after dinner," the doctor said.

Jack was glad Vicki had gone to check on the corn and hadn't heard him use the word *betray*. When she joined them back on the deck, Jack asked Vicki if she would get him another beer.

"Why? Your leg broken, hon?"

"Bring me one, too," the doctor told Jack.

They ate around a redwood picnic table with a pole poked through the center for an umbrella. There were pink flamingos on the plastic tumblers and chili peppers painted on the rims of the plates. "In a year or so," the doctor said, "we'll have a swimming pool to look out onto."

Their aging dog, Banker, grayed at the temples and muzzle, with his air of a retired cruise director, got up from under the table to check out the new dog that had moved in next door. Jack and the doctor got going about the Knicks until Vicki mimed the act of sawing, sawing off her place from their part of the table. She had learned the gesture from Jack. When she had his attention, she said, "I want you to see my friend Trina. It's not like that—she's a psychic."

Vicki's favorite subject after feelings was the paranormal.

"You know, I bribed the doctor here to go to a hypnotist to quit smoking," she said. "If he'd have given it a chance, it might have worked."

"The guy didn't swing a watch on a chain," the doctor told Jack. "He just talked to me really slowly. He *bored* me into a half-trance, something you know I can get at any goddamn dinner party."

"Trina has movie star clients," Vicki said. "She looks like a movie star herself. She'll come to your house."

"I had an out-of-body experience before I left," Jack said, playing with her. "And it was good," he said, reflective, " 'cause I could help myself pack."

Vicki stood up to clear the table.

"It looks like Vicki here is doing all the work," the doctor pointed out.

Jack leaned back in his chair and drawled, "*I* have no problem with Vicki doing all the work."

"Jack?"

"Vick?"

"I used to think a lot of you."

She brought out a stack of dessert plates and a string-tied bakery box. "You want to do a line of pie?"

"Dogs heard you," the doctor said. Banker had returned from telling off the neighbors for starting their car. He had with him the puppy from next door, a clumsy mutt named Boss that it had fallen to Vicki to train.

"He's been gaining a pound a day," Vicki said, admiring.

"He's a miracle of cell division," the doctor said, scooting him over to Jack.

Jack examined the pup's chest and belly. "Where do the batteries go?"

Over bourbon-pecan pie, Vicki asked about the breakup and Jack tried to change the subject. When she prefaced a remark with "She wasn't nice enough to me not to tell you this," Jack could tell she was in his corner.

None of it was news to him, but he could hear what Vicki was saying. Not understand "where she was coming from"—he could literally hear her voice. Toward the end, he hadn't been able to hear his wife. When he asked her a question and cared about the answer, he could not seem to keep his attention fixed on her. "What do you mean?" he would say to Alex and hope she would repeat the gist of it.

Jack didn't have to say anything to Vicki because, at their feet, the puppy let pass audible gas.

"The bloom is off the rose," Jack said.

"The plug is on the nose," the doctor said. Both men waved their hands in front of their faces.

A beetle flew into Vicki's cleavage; she stood to flick it out, and the doctor said you couldn't blame it for trying.

Jack said, "What movie star does your psychic friend look like tomorrow?"

Jack woke to the sound of his car alarm. He went to the kitchen to look out on to the driveway and found Vicki leaning on a counter, laughing.

"You missed it," she said. "Boss went over to pee on your tire? He lifted his leg and set off the alarm and toppled right over."

Jack disconnected the alarm—Boss had hidden in shame—and went back inside the house for coffee.

Vicki was running a roll of masking tape up and down an arm of her cardigan, picking up fur. She handed it to Jack to do her back. She said, "Breakfast?"

"What've we got?"

"If we had some ham we could have ham and eggs—" Vicki said, and waited for Jack to join her on "if we had some eggs."

Jack looked at her samples of countertop materials— a kitchen renovation was next—and watched her chop a pepper for an eggless omelette.

"There are appliances that do that for you."

"But I hate to move into the twentieth or twenty-first century, whichever this is," Vicki said, and reached to turn up a song of busted romance that was on the kitchen radio. Jack listened until an ad for some lame kind of career came on. He had a small graphics business that ran itself; every ad he saw or heard made him think: Is this what I'm supposed to do next?

Vicki worked three days a week at the hospital as a physical therapist, sometimes carrying out her husband's instructions. She taught people how to walk again, helped them recover a grip. She gave a surpassing deep-heat massage, the doctor told Jack, and Vicki herself had several times offered this to him. Jack had been afraid he might *respond* and embarrass them both, so had always begged off. But this morning, when she saw him straining to look over his shoulder at the dogs, he let her work on the back of his neck.

When she finished, he said, "I've got something for you."

He opened his gym bag and took a tiny box out of a zippered nylon pocket. Inside, under a layer of cotton, were gold earrings that each framed a piece of round onyx in the center.

"You have pierced ears, right?" he said.

"I love them," Vicki said, putting them on. She moved to a hallway mirror and pulled her tangled hair away from her face.

"They came with blue stones or red ones, too," Jack said. "The salesgirl kept pushing me to get a color, but I'm a big black man." He snorted and said, "Yeah, I'm Denzel Washington."

Vicki touched her ears and turned from side to side for Jack to see. "Trina's coming at two," she told him. "I'll be out of the way."

"What do I do with her?" Jack said.

"*She'll* tell *you*," Vicki said, and left for the hospital.

Jack was wearing a T-shirt Alex had brought him from last year's sales conference. It said across the front: THE DANTEL GROUP COMMITMENT TO EXCELLENCE 1993. His gym bag said: the DANTEL GROUP THE LEADERSHIP ADVANTAGE

1992, and—no telling why since they didn't have a child—there was a baby's bib in the glove compartment with another go-getter slogan. (Nineteen-eighty-nine—BUILDING ON THE BEST—was the only year in their years together that Alex hadn't brought Jack back a souvenir. That was the year the company had tried to cut corners. Alex's budget for the conference had been reduced, and the motivational speaker she'd been able to afford was the backup quarterback for a losing team. He had, it turned out, one speech for all occasions and had earnestly urged the management team of The Dan'lel Group to "stay in school.")

Jack hoped he had one clean T-shirt left. He had packed up a box of his clothes to take along, but instead of loading it into the car, he had left it beside a Dumpster, saying, "This'll show *me!* This shirt I wore last summer?—I won't be wearing *it* again."

Jack shaved and put on an old blue shirt that Alex had told him played up his own blue eyes. He worked a snakeskin belt that belonged to the doctor through the loops of his jeans, then took it off in case it scrambled signals to the psychic. He practiced a clear countenance in the mirror, reminded himself that this was not a date, and smoked a joint while watching a sports roundup show on TV.

The psychic, who was only as spooky as any beautiful girl, had barely had time to begin when Alex called from California to tell Jack that her mother had had a stroke. Jack asked if she wanted him to come back, but Alex said no, she wanted to talk to him was all.

Jack apologized to the psychic as he walked her to the door. He asked if he could take her to dinner the next night in lieu of a reading.

"What are you doing with a psychic?" Alex asked.

"Vicki set it up," Jack said.

"She say anything about us?" Alex said. "Not Vicki, the psychic?"

"Trina," Jack said. "She said my departed cousin Barry is still looking out for me."

"You *hated* Barry," Alex said. "*Barry's* looking out for you?"

"She said he was in the room with us," Jack told Alex. "I told her to get him out of there!"

Jack didn't tell Alex that he had invited the psychic to dinner. They talked about her mother, who had been as much his mother as hers.

"Alex," Jack said after a while, "we've managed to talk for an hour without either one of us crying."

And Alex said, "Hang up right now."

When she had recovered, she phoned Jack back. She was wistful and reminiscent, as though her mother's life had already ended. Alex said her mother was the oldest person kids called by her first name. She said she had so many friends, and always remembered which sorrow went with which person. Jack said their friends from high school, when they came back to visit their parents, always called on *her* mother, too.

When the conversation ended, Jack thought about

all the things he hadn't seen coming. He walked the residential streets until dark, saw timed lights lighting and dimming, controlled by preset clocks.

The next day: "What did you think of Trina?" Vicki said.

"High marks," Jack said, "but there's still the long program and the free skating." He almost told Vicki what he hadn't told Alex, that the psychic had predicted a turbulent year ahead with the love of his life.

Vicki was assembling an ambitious salad of smoked trout and red lettuce and grapefruit—substituted, she said, for a citrus type of fruit you couldn't get in this country.

Earlier, Jack had heard her on the phone with the doctor; he heard her say "setback" and thought they were talking about him till he could tell they were talking about a patient.

"Me, me, me," Jack had chanted to himself.

He looked at the French cookbook she'd left open on the counter, and said, "Cauliflower *Grenobloise?*"

"I've made it before," Vicki said. "It's not as throw-uppy as it sounds."

Without looking up from her work, she said, "Not that I'm pushing you out the door, but I was thinking we should get you some books on tape for when you drive home."

"You don't think they're kind of dangerous?" Jack said. "I'm listening to the book and it's a really good part when I reach the house, so I pull into the garage and close the door and keep the car running to find out what happens and they find me in the car the next morning dead?"

Vicki handed him a jar of seedy mustard sealed with wax. "Can you do this for me?"

Jack opened the jar, then poured himself a scotch. He tore off the corner of a bag of cheese-flavored popcorn, summoning Banker and Boss. The dogs had been napping in the herb garden, and came inside wagging thyme, basil and dill through the kitchen. Jack flicked kernels at the older dog, who caught them with a snap in the air. *The clean way a dog enlists your heart,* he thought.

Vicki mixed a vinaigrette and joined him, minus the scotch. She tried in vain to control the pup. "You can't train a dog with popcorn flying through the air," Jack said.

"Then give it a rest," Vicki said to Jack. "Watch this."

She got the puppy to sit but couldn't get him to lie down. She tried to ask a question about Alex's mother, but the puppy wanted to play, so her question was spliced and punctuated with commands—"Do you DOWN think you will NO go to California SIT to be with Alex?"—a kind of canine Tourette's.

"Everyone's out there now," Jack said. "It's later she'll maybe need help."

"What about you?"

"I always need help," Jack said, and reached across the table for the smaller of the local papers. He turned to the "Tide Table" and, with a couple of hours before he had to pick up Trina, asked Vicki if she wanted to take the dogs to the beach.

Jack picked up the car keys when Vicki came out of her bedroom pulling on a large faded work shirt over a modest one-piece bathing suit. Vicki opened the tailgate of her station wagon, and Banker jumped in. The puppy whimpered until Vicki bent over and lifted him.

It was late enough in the day that they had most of the beach to themselves. Jack surveyed the surf as they hopped across still-hot sand; he said, "Look- -the bluefish are running!"

Bluefish churned the water in a feeding frenzy. Closer up, Jack and Vicki could see two-footers leaping, roiling in the waves not six feet from the sand, scaring up bait fish onto the shore. There was no stepping around them, the sudden numbers of them, so that fish wiggled inside sandals, fish were under their feet, inside of their shoes and they had to unbuckle those shoes and make squeamish faces as they held the shoes away from their bodies and the thin silver bait fish, inches long, rained to the sand.

"The bluefish in a school, do they know one another?" This from Vicki, who did not wait for an answer but hooted at Jack to look at Banker, who was sitting at attention a few feet out to sea with the tail of a fish waving up and down in his mouth until with one intake of breath the dog sucked the fish in and gulped it down.

Jack was instantly giddy with fish. He scooped up

handfuls of fish and, fast as he could, hurled them back into the water as though their lives were not already over.

Vicki gathered shells that she scattered in the garden when they got home. She threw wet towels across the picnic table to dry.

In the shower, watching sand wash down the drain, Jack recalled the psychic's prediction of a turbulent year ahead, and it struck him that the psychic had not said that Alex was the love of his life. He had *assumed* that was who she was talking about.

This made him happy. "I am started," he quoted the old poem, "the tugs have left me."

He was ready for whatever the psychic could tell him. He wanted to be told what was coming and where he had been. And if you had to, he reasoned, there was nothing wrong with faking your way to where you belonged.

Trina was shorter than Jack remembered. She had, therefore, to look up at a man, exposing her throat, which was unadorned but for the deep V of a V-necked dress to entice the eye down.

"I thought we'd go into the city," Jack said, and headed back onto the expressway where, for the ten remaining miles, they had a view of the skyline at dusk.

Jack said, "The city looks pretty good."

The psychic said, "Give it a minute."

Housewife

She would always sleep with her husband and with another man in the course of the same day, and then the rest of the day, for whatever was left to her of that day, she would exploit by incanting, "*French* film, *French* film."

The Annex

The headlights hit the headstone and I hate it all over again. It is all that I can ever see, all that I can ever talk about. There is nothing else to talk about.

It is right there out in front. I mean the cemetery that is out over there across the street from our house. With the headlights turned off and the car parked outside the garage, there is enough of a moon to see that there is no missing it over there across the street in the part of the cemetery the people around here call the annex.

The annex is for when the cemetery fills up.

Anyway, there is a stone there that has the baby's name on it. And there was a week-old bouquet of something all dried up past knowing what it was that was tied with wide white ribbon out there until the time I came home today. There was a white ribbon on it. I could have taken the ribbon away. But the woman would have come and put another one, I suppose.

This is a cemetery which has its shapely tended trees and flowerful shrubs and Halloween headstones that go back two hundred years. The thing that is different about the annex is that the annex is not landscaped. It is a wild grown-over field of scrub oak and dune grass that gets bulldozed and plowed under as the need, in somebody's mind, arises, one row at a time. Except that the men who run the bulldozers and things don't call what they are clearing a row.

I made a point of finding out.

They call it a plot line.

From every window in the front of our house, when you look out, that gravestone is what you see—from the sunporch, from the living room, from the dining room, from the bedroom upstairs, from the garage where my husband and I have been cleaning out the junk that belonged to the previous owners, which is why I cannot now find the shovel when I reach up to the place where it should be.

There is every other kind of tool hanging from nails pounded in. My husband is good at all the housey things that require these bucksaws and shingling hammers and extension ladders, the pitchfork and pruning shears, the lazy boy, the pick.

You see what it is? It is a two-car garage with a loft where we haven't had time yet to make the big effort to clean out the crap from the previous owners, why didn't they clean out their own crap, is what I want to know.

The oversized stuffed animals, the rotten throw pillows, the mildewed best-sellers from other summers, everything cheap and ruined and left behind.

Where is the shovel?

Can you believe it? The flowers were baby's breath.

I wanted to ask my husband if you call it a baby at the age of five months.

I mean five *unborn* months!

According to him, my husband, the date on the stone is only the month and the year. But I have not crossed the street to see if that is really what the stone says.

I can tell you it's got an arch across the top. But no cherubs that I can see.

And I can see.

For days after the burial, I would go inside the house, leaving weeds unpulled in the border of portulaca; I would leave the hose coupling loose and spitting, and hide out in the kitchen while the woman visited the site. I would pour myself a glass of lemonade and carry it into the dining room and look across the street to where the woman had parked her rental car and was standing there looking at her dead baby.

She came with some new flowers today. I saw her come with them. They are a big bunch of purple cosmos. Local—what's in bloom right now.

The other thing she did was plant a row of impatiens that I happen to know will not last any time at all in this heat.

She would know it too if she actually lived around here.

Well, she doesn't, thank God.

Something else, which is that she was wearing a sweater that I could tell was from a catalog that I had just been looking at that I myself get in the mail, too. I could see the ribbing at the neck and wrists. She was wearing it in plum. I was going to order it in black.

Was.

Although black is not a very smart color to wear around here. Not with the dust that is forever finding its way onto everything I wear. Not when you have to go into a filthy garage with its leftover heaps of plastic crap.

What did he use the shovel for last?

To move our scraps onto the compost pile, chances are. But he would not have left the shovel outside, would he? He is careful with tools. He is careful, and he has a good eye. He was the one who kept me from throwing out the one good thing the previous owners left behind—an ice bucket with a procession of penguins marching right around the middle of it.

There was a high chair left behind in the garage, too. It was a pretty good one, I suppose—if you could get yourself not to see Donald Duck saying "Let's eat!" painted on it. The lousy thing was that he cleaned it up and drove it over to the house she was going to rent for the summer. I suppose he thought it would be a useful thing for her to have for when she had the baby. Well, she never had it!

Maybe he should have also taken over the chess set the previous owners left behind. I mean, you never can tell about babies, can you.

I bet we never get the high chair back. Someone who buries her baby in your front yard is not going to think to give you back anything you ever lent her. Not that she'd have to go out of her way to do it. I mean, she's there every day—at the annex, that is.

And now our dog goes over there to bark at her when she comes.

She's usually happy to just tag along with us around the yard as we garden. She likes to dig in the dirt, nap in the sun. The usual. At the end of each day we walk her across the street and through the annex to a pond beyond the cemetery where she swims out under a covered bridge to fetch her ball and sticks. We don't want the dog to cross the street without us, but that is what she does when there is a person who gets out of a car and stands there so close by.

When we first moved here, we didn't know the streetlight was going to shine in our bedroom window. Is this why we're up so much—because of the light? Or is it because we know that I have what she already had and still wants?

I can almost believe that somewhere is the person who could look across the street and see a vision of perfect peace, the resting place of someone who, unlike the rest of us, was only encouraged and adored.

When sunlight hits the headstone so, it flashes through the branches of the copper beech we planted to obscure it. If I stare long enough, it will burn a hole through my head.

For the rest of my habitation in this house, in this marriage, her baby will be buried in my life unless I can make my way to back behind the stacks of shingles and to back behind the row of storm doors and to back behind the rolled hammock—and maybe find the goddamn shovel.

The New Lodger

One of the locals said at the bar, "I hear you've got a new lodger." I thought, Word travels fast—I only got here last night.

In a corner booth of the Soggy Dollar, an old beach bar that also serves food, I can listen to other customers without seeming to eavesdrop; I've got postcards fanned out on the table. I'm trying not to say the same thing on every one.

The best is an aerial view of the road you take to get here. Seeing this ahead of time, you would choose to go somewhere else. Hugging the inside curves of the road, taking steady deep breaths, I can drive myself here, but not back. I hire one of the locals to drive my car down to the junction of the road where I can take over. I arrange for a taxi to meet us there, and I cover the large fare back.

"It's imported," the bartender says, and pours a glass for the guy at the bar who meant *lager.*

"What do you think?" the bartender says. "Should I order more?"

It is not easy to get to this beach. The one road is dangerous even in good weather, even during the day. It winds around the hills on the edge of a cliff, climbing above the ocean until it suddenly grades down. People have lost their lives on the way to this beach, or on their way home from it. Heading home puts you in the outer lane where there is no guard rail, not that it would help. There is only the occasional turnout for a scenic lookout point, and people mindful of others pull over to let them pass.

It's a moody beach, more often foggy than bright. It is rarely warm enough to take a swim. It is pretty to look at, the cove a perfect C, and there's the haunted house tour if you're that hard up. For excitement: the peril of a storm that washes away a residence, fire in the dry hills, a fight that breaks out among bikers passing through. The new lager.

I hadn't been to this town since the time, years before, when I nearly drowned. I credit the pancakes I'd had that morning for giving me something to draw on to fight the current, until I remembered not to fight the current, but to swim parallel to land until I had swum past the current and could then turn in toward shore.

I took a room in the annex to the Soggy Dollar that had not been built the last time I was here.

The first time I saw this beach was with a man who, during our stay, compared himself to Jesus, so the trip had not been a waste of time for him. Someone else brought me the second time. We rented, for a day, a cabin across from the beach with atmosphere and damp chairs. I told him it was my birthday. He left me in the cabin, and came back carrying a piece of chocolate cake. There were no plates or forks. He watched me as I ate the cake. I said, "What—am I covered with frosting?" "Every day of your life," he said, and went home to his wife.

The third time I had those pancakes.

I'll stay for as long as it takes. I will not get in touch with anyone on my list. Not the friends of friends who live nearby, whose gardens I must see, whose children I must meet. Nor will I visit the famed nature preserve, home of a vanishing tern. Why get acquainted with what will be left, or leaving?

Farther up the coast is where you have to go for stuffed plush whales and orange rubber crabs, for T-shirts and mugs, placemat maps. Postcards are what the store can manage. That's okay with me. I don't have to hunt up souvenirs. It is enough to feel the pull of the old home, pulling apart the new.

Tumble Home

. . . I would have traded
places with anyone raised on love,
but how would anyone raised on love
bear this death?

—Sharon Olds, from "Wonder"

I have written letters that are failures, but I have written
few, I think, that are lies. Trying to reach a person means
asking the same question over and again: Is this the
truth, or not? I begin this letter to you, then, in the western tradition. If I understand it, the western tradition is:
Put your cards on the table.

This is easier, I think, when your life has been tipped
over and poured out. Things matter less; there is the joy
of being less polite, and of being less—not more—careful. We can say everything.

Although maybe not. Like in fishing? The lighter the
line, the easier it is to get your lure down deep. Having

delivered myself of the manly analogy, I see it to be not a failure, but a lie. How can I possibly put an end to this when it feels so good to pull sounds out of my body and show them to you. These sounds—this letter—it is my lipstick, my lingerie, my high heels.

Writing to you fills the days in this place. And sometimes I long for days when nothing happens. "Not every clocktick needs a martyr."

The trees are all on crutches, on sawed-off braces of deadwood notched into Y-shaped crooks for support. The birds that nest in these crippled trees line their nests with the clumps of fur that come loose to float over brambled grass when the house cat is groomed out of doors. The birds are fat on seeds that did not flower. Seed packets mark our places in books. Everyone here is better than they were there, "there" being anywhere else. The fact of someplace else means we are not native. Not one of us started here first.

What got me here was a six, according to the nurse who had devised her own scale. And I remember thinking, What must be the sevens and eights if this is only a six?

I have killed two of the wrong things to kill. It is not like the city where you know what to kill. First a preying mantis (they will eat the other bugs if you give them a chance to do it) and then a firefly which, without its glow, was just a beetle in the bathroom.

Some of those of us who stay here appreciate the trend toward doctors calling their patients "guests." But I think I would be happy to wear a plastic bracelet and a white gown that fails to cover my backside. Patients, guests, we are expected to get well enough to leave, even if it is only for an afternoon drive. When I get a pass and a car comes to pick me up, what I have the driver do is park across the street from the gate so that I have this place in sight until it is time for me to come back. The driver can keep the radio on if he likes—or if she does. All I want is to see where I'm going next.

A pass is a formality; we can leave anytime we want. I usually call a car, but others take the bus into town. The time I took the bus, I felt sure that if the side of my face were to touch the window glass, the skin would be abraded, and I spent the duration of the ride leaning into the window.

At a famous institute of technology there is a room filled with scale-model trains set up to run in perpetuity through a scale model of the town that is home to the institute. You can watch the trains power along the tracks and through the tunnels and avoid near-collisions before you notice the clock on the wall and its madly spinning hands.

The clock is on scale time, of course.

Those of us who have to leave here, even briefly, feel, I think, that time, anywhere else, is like this—like scale time.

What goes on when things go well: I see Warren pushing the house cat "out to sea" on the Styrofoam cover of the ice chest on the pond. I brush a shed hair from my collar and the hair turns out to be cornsilk.

There is the unidentified object that flies. When any one of us spots it hovering above the house, we all grab a book and run to the lawn and hold up the books to show them what kind of people we are.

Shakespeare and Tolstoy!

Run get Jane Austen!

If you take the highway to get here, you will pass our favorite sign. Posted at the entrance to the housing development a few miles back, the sign says, RESIDENTIAL HOMES. Some of the residential homes are under construction still. We like the smell of cut lumber, the way post and beam meet, the men working so fast, cobwebs can't form in the eaves.

The Southerner among us is Chatten Gaines. She will take a chair in the sun and produce a bottle of lotion, her Swiss Performing Extract, and Warren will ask, "What does it do—cartwheels?" Chatty will say to watch out he doesn't become an outpatient.

The definition of outpatient here is: a person who has fainted, who has passed *out*.

I believe that moisturizing has become as important to Chatty as accessorizing—that retail verb. I can tell you that both activities are crucial to me.

*   *   *

The vegetable garden is open to us all, and all are encouraged to cultivate something in it. Consequently, there are rows of trendy lettuce, beans climbing poles tied up like tepees, tiny yellow tomatoes shaped like lightbulbs, kale not even the moles will eat, and my own contribution—nothing so literal as a vegetable, but row after row of perfect dwarf zinnias. This is not bragging; given the soil here, you can shake the seeds out like salt on a baked potato, tamp not a spicule of soil on top of them, and up they will come to a height greater than you would want.

I am not quite myself, I think.

But who here is quite himself? And yet there is a way in which we all are more ourselves than ever, I suppose.

I have made friends with the Southerner. Chatty is not one of those ironic nicknames as when a fat person is known as "Tiny." Chatty says that when she was a girl away at school and the holidays were coming, her mother would ask if she was bringing home any listeners. Chatty talks about the poltergeist and what will it do next—turn up the stereo in the music room, run an upstairs shower, turn on the fan above the stove if it doesn't like the smell of our dinner cooking?

The nearest neighbor is not so near. Still, you can hear

his country music, faint from down the road, till all hours of night. The nearest neighbor is from the South, and how he knows if he likes you is he puts on Hank Williams and do you know who that is singing? Coming in so low when you are lying in bed awake—it is the pleasure of keeping the radio on all night when you were just able to have a friend stay over, and all you cared to drink in the dark was ginger ale.

Sometimes in the dark a person will call out, "Where am I?" and really want to know. What must be the nines and tens?

Have you noticed there are no second sheets? I use the blue letter paper with my name at the top of *every* page. I do this because of a dream I had the first night I was here. In the dream, I went to pick up the stationery I had ordered for myself in waking life. But in the dream, there was a different name at the top of each sheet.

I did not have to puzzle over what this meant. Those people whose names were on my stationery? It seems to me that I am every one of them.

Writing to you, I am myself. And what that self is I will tell you: a graveyard. I can be a graveyard. But that is a thing you would have to find out for yourself. A person cannot tell you a thing and have you just believe them. A person has to prove it. You would find out, if you cared to, that I have told no one about you. As if anyone would believe me if I had! As I think you would be the first to agree, it is hard to know what to believe anymore.

Although this is the kind of place that can call your bluff. It's like—let's say you are at a mixer in high school, and a boy you don't like keeps asking you to dance. Let's say he keeps coming over, and each time he asks, you say, "Let's wait for a good one." Then "Great Balls of Fire" comes on, and what are you going to say—"I'm waiting for 'Color My World'?"

This place was once a school for girls. For one hundred years a tony school for girls in the Georgian style with a circular drive, then mounting fiscal problems and a merger with the corresponding school for boys, only the name retained in the hyphenated name of the new institution.

After many years vacant, what was once a parlor hung with portraits of the founder, the place the girls received their guests, is now a lounge we call the Hostility Suite. The paint is fresh, the armchairs inviting, the wood polished; it stops short of fussy. It is easy to imagine mattresses being pulled off the beds upstairs, and teenaged girls in baby-doll pajamas surfing them down the stairs.

And how about this for the way life works—one of the patients used to be a student. When Chatty was away at school, this was the school she went to until she was kicked out, that is, for drinking. She plays the drinking down, says she monitored herself using the Jimi Hendrix test: Am I choking on my own vomit? No? Then I can have another drink.

Chatty has lost nearly all of her short-term memory, and she loves it. Wasn't that the point, she asks, of drinking? But she says her recollections of school are untouched. She said a platinum screen goddess had attended in the thirties, and had sneaked out through the chapel to elope. Chatty said that every girl in the school for years after claimed that the screen star's room was her own.

Chatty remembers jumping out of her window and running to the beach where, under a full moon, you could make shadows on the sand. She said she sabotaged convocations, substituting vegetable seeds for the flowers in the Centennial Garden, so that where should have bloomed hollyhocks—corn stalks. And in place of delphiniums, butternut squash.

School had not been, for me, the place of unalloyed joy and fulfillment that it was for her. When the other girls squealed, "Let's jump in the car and go have hijinks," I was the one who asked, "How far is the car?" If deferred to in any way, I would go up in a bonfire of self-immolation. Now here we both are. And I am writing to you.

I have to roll up my sleeves to do so.

Did you wonder why my clothes were too big? Why I kept having to push up the sleeve of my sweater to lift my cup of tea? This is a holdover from high school, from when I read in a women's magazine that to make yourself look small, you should wear your clothes too big. The column went on—it said don't stop there! It said buy yourself oversized furniture so as to look small and delicate when curled up in a chair.

Are you wondering why a person who is already small would want to make herself look smaller? That should become clear. Not everything I know is something I want to see. Though on highways and, once, on a mountain road, I have strained to see things I didn't want to see. The worst I ever saw was a body without a head. That was when I realized that I don't mind seeing everything as long as everything is there for me to see.

The person I strained to see on the mountain road was myself. A paramedic wouldn't let me. He cut away my jacket and sweater, then he scissored off my shirt. It seemed to me he could have covered me up faster than he did. In the hospital, a doctor laid his hand on my shoulder. Does this hurt? he asked. Moving his hand to my collarbone, What about here? And lower. Does this feel good?

It felt like that joke that I can't exactly remember, but that has to do with a woman being examined in a doctor's office. I think the way it goes is that after the naked woman has been thoroughly examined, she asks what is wrong with her. And the man in the white coat says he wouldn't know, he's not the doctor.

When someone starts heading for the life they had before, Chatty says, "Steam your face." She herself will lean over a pot of boiling water with a towel held tented over her head and over the pot. She puts chamomile leaves in the boiling water and says the effect is soothing. But chamomile is the tea you drank that day, and the scent of it here is too much for me.

I lost my watch the day we met. Without a watch, to find the time I pick up the remote and turn on the weather channel. Trying to find the time, I track tornadoes in the plains states. A lost watch is something I will have to look up. I, who above and beyond the normal precautions, make fortune-courting gestures such as placing my shoes at my bedroom door with one shoe pointing in and one shoe pointing out—this to prevent nightmares—although it makes me look as though I don't know whether I am coming or going. I am superstitious, and never change the bed sheets on a Friday (it gives the devil control of your dreams). When I wanted to measure your intentions when you agreed to meet me for tea, I threw apple pips into a fire and said, "If you love me, pop and fly, if you hate me, lay and die." A lost watch is something I will have to look up. I am superstitious, and sometimes confused, opening an umbrella before I leave the house, but never, ever, wearing sunglasses inside.

A fetish for me, sunglasses, so I was glad that you said you liked the green ones. "Show me what else you've got in there"—when I put the glasses back in my bag, how nicely you cued me up. Show me what else you've got in there. Because the last time someone said that to me, it was a gorilla that said it, the one who talks in sign language with her hands. She said the same thing to me—I sat as close to her, a famous gorilla, as I sat to you—after she, too, admired my green-rimmed glasses. I think you could see that, had you let me, I would have talked about that gorilla till brooms were thrust under our feet. The situation is this: if you stopped people on the street and asked how they felt about gorillas, I would be among the ones who lighted right up.

And she said with her hands, "Show me what else you've got in there." For her, I took out everything I had and held it up so she could say to me with her hands, "Pretty"—the green-rimmed glasses, and "Put on"—a tube of lipstick! And when I held up an invitation to an opening (not one of yours), at a gallery, held it up so she could see the side of the card that showed the artist's work, "Lousy painting" is what she signed! Because she paints, too. I wish I could tell people here that you said to that, "They all do."

I would have told you about how, when it was time for me to leave, she asked me with her hands to stay, but it was enough that you said, "I envy you your gorilla."

I warn you: Don't get me started on dogs! Volunteers from the shelter arrive with orphaned dogs to walk. Karen has become loquacious, but only when a dog is present. On the days the dogs come, Karen sings the same song, only changing the words to fit each newcomer: "Sad-eyed Mongrel (Mastiff, Shepherd) of the Lowlands."

Since the dogs began to visit, Karen has been going to

chapel. There, although she does not have religion, she lights a candle—"for Saint Bernard," she says, her only joke.

The dogs from the shelter take a great deal of pleasure in pissing on pine needles and lapping at mud puddles when you volunteer to walk them in the woods behind the pound. We can do this sometimes. Karen has become enamored of the shelter's mascot, a dog who, because of his age, is unlikely to be adopted. Banker came to visit once, but frightened another guest, so every day that she is allowed, Karen drags a vinyl chair across the concrete floor and positions it in front of Banker's cage when the weather is too bad for her to take him outside.

In the first flush of companionship, Karen and Banker had rolled in the woods, and Karen, careless in a sleeveless blouse, had found patches of rash from poison ivy crusting into epaulettes on her shoulders.

Sometimes I go with her to the shelter, and that is how I heard about the job that she lost. She said a dove was walking north on Madison Avenue, walking with a limp, when it turned left at 73rd Street and entered Pierre Deux. Karen was on her way to a job interview, but she followed the bird into the store. The bird was hurt, that was clear, so Karen said she wrapped it in a remnant of French challis and took it to the hospital known as the Mayo Clinic for animals. She said she wrote out a check for the bird's costly treatment, then put it in a cab for Brooklyn where there is a sanctuary for such cases. She took the driver's number, told him the person at the other end would call her when he arrived.

She said she missed her interview. So did this make her compassionate, Karen asked, or just ambivalent?

Banker had gone from a sit to lying down. The dog's eyes remained on Karen the entire time. When she finished speaking, he thumped his tail.

"Good boy," Karen said.

A young woman came over to the pen with a large plastic scoop. She opened Banker's kennel and removed his dish, filled it with food and put it back in the part of the kennel that was unroofed and open to the air. The woman left to tend the other dogs, and Karen spoke to Banker; she said it was exhausting to always have two jobs—your job, and the job of being able to do your job in the first place.

A blue jay dove into Banker's bowl and flew off with a kibble from his dinner.

"How do you do both?"

My guess was you worked twice as hard, but I wasn't the one she asked.

Only Warren can pull her out of a mood. Last night she told us she was going to go look at a litter of puppies. Warren told her there was no such thing as "just looking" at puppies.

"Often you *do* see puppies that just aren't cute enough," he said. Then he wondered aloud what kind of puppy did we think Karen could pass up. "Let's see," he said in Karen's voice, "all the internal organs are on the outside? I can live with that."

"I like golden retrievers," Karen said.

"You don't think they've kind of got that Stepford thing going?" Warren said.

Warren is pronounced Warn, or Worn.

You know how most of us don't say things in a memorable way? The way everything sounds already *handled* by everyone else? But Warren says, when he is angry, that he's as mad as all outdoors. He says do I want to meet him after dinner and chew the rug? He says he can't always follow the threat of my conversation.

When Chatty sees Warren in her old school dorm, she says she nearly calls out, "Man on the floor!"

I think you would like Warren. He drinks Courvoisier in a Coke can, and has a laugh like you'd find in a cartoon balloon.

Sometimes we go into town together. Last time, we got a ride in with the gardener. He had to stop at the Ford dealership to pick up a part for the van, and I followed Warren into the car repair dock. Warren took a cigarette out of his pack, and a uniformed employee said, "No smoking, sir. They don't let us smoke here." Warren took out a pack of matches and lit his cigarette. "But *you* can smoke. You're a customer," the mechanic said. Warren flicked his used match into the lube bay and looked straight at the guy. "I guess if *I* buy a truck here, I can smoke too," the guy said.

That was the day before Warren's parents came to visit. They were coming from a small town in Texas. I told him I looked forward to meeting them, even though it always seemed that the very things others find charming about your parents—the feyness, the provincialism, the odd takes on everything—are the things that make you want to rustle up a firing squad.

Warren smoked his cigarette, held it low on his lip. At dinner the first night, Chatty had said in my ear that if Jean-Paul Belmondo had not been born, Warren would not have had a personality. She said it was hard not to notice that it was a long way from Belmondo to Warren Moore.

He pulled a folded snapshot from the pocket of his canvas pants. It was an aerial view of a small island. The island was shaped like a heart.

"They came to my island in the spring," he said, of the last time he'd seen his parents, "when everything was in bloom and I had cleaned up the house. They were supposed to stay a week, but after two days, my mother said they had to go home. She hadn't liked anything about it," Warren said, "not the ride on my boat, not even that I had rigged a pot at the end of the pier and dropped the shrimp into boiling water the minute I fished them out of the ocean. I called her back in Texas. I said, 'Dad was here last week, and he brought your evil twin.' "

The gardener had dropped us at the plant store. Warren had said he wanted to find a book on bulbs. Did he plan to be here to see fall-planted bulbs bloom next spring? The plant store is next door to a shuttered-by-day gay bar called Manhandlers. The owner of the bar also owns the plant store, which is why Warren calls it Planthandlers. He said it made him feel funny when he went in to buy tomatoes, and had to ask the owner for "Big Boys" and "Beefmaster."

Warren paid for his book. I looked at the back of his hands where intravenous drips had left tiny scars like age spots. We all have them.

The gardener came to fetch us that day toting a paper bag filled with dozens of packs of gum. He handed a couple of packs to each of us. He said it was for the moles in the garden, that we had to chew the gum, then put it down their holes because the moles like the taste and would eat it but couldn't digest it and it would kill them. He said he was also going to try those plastic pinwheels that you can get at carnivals, that those were supposed to work, too. Vibrations sent into the ground by the pinwheel spinning at the end of the stick.

We left Planthandlers with gum in our mouths. Outside, at the entrance to the greenhouse, a dog licked crumbs of fertilizer off the blade of a shovel.

When he is ready, Warren will return to his heart-shaped island. He says he can't wait, but he is waiting.

A thing I haven't told anyone is that *this* place is the place where I feel the way you would feel on a heart-shaped island, glad to open my eyes from dreams of the place I live where the boys next door are dim malevolent twins who ride their bicycles onto my lawn and say, when I go out to shoo them away, "We know you from somewhere." "You know me from right here," is what I tell them, and go back inside.

Tumble home. It's a shipbuilding term I learned from Warren. It's the place on a ship that is, if I understand him, the widest part of the bow before it narrows to cut through water—it is the point where the water parts and goes to one side of the ship or the other. To me, the tumble home is the place where nothing can touch you.

I have walked barefoot on floors so badly cleaned I had to brush off my feet before sliding them between the sheets at night. Floors cleaned not at all is what I mean, because the cleaning was left to me.

Here it's not my job so the floors are clean. Our rooms, Chatty says, are the same as years before. There are no college pennants tacked up on the walls, no posters of rock stars, either. Just serviceable furniture—a maple chest and desk, a single bed refreshed by the linen service weekly, and hangers that cannot be removed from the closet, a hotel touch. At the end of each hall is a kitchenette with baskets of apples and oranges, and packets of hot chocolate mix.

We can personalize the rooms to the extent we care to. Chatty hung curtains of crocheted lace, but I like a room that doesn't give a person away. Though I do display a collage I made. It is a photograph of a Great Dane looking at his leg where I strapped on a photo of a Timex to his wrist. The title of this piece is "Watchdog Watching." We're all artists here.

Would it make you uneasy to know that I have seen the inside of your house? Anyone who bought that magazine did. It surprised me. I would have guessed you lived in spare rooms done in stinging whites and grays. But there you were by a cozy fire in a house more lodge than stage. And in the studio where you paint: orderly racks of canvases, the wood-burning stove to heat the place. But is it a good idea to have an ax in the room where you work?

And a swimming pool in the backyard. I never had a swimming pool; I swam in a willow-ringed pond. My favorite thing was staying in the longest when a thunderstorm struck (*She is the smallest child who swings the highest* my mother once wrote in a letter to my father). What can I say about myself today? That I am the last to close a window when it rains.

I am writing now beside an open window in Little Egypt. When this was school, Chatty said, they called the smoker Little Egypt because of all the Camels in it. They blew their smoke out the window that overlooks the circular drive and from which we can see everyone arrive and leave.

Little Egypt is to the second floor what the Hostility Suite is to the first floor, only gamier. I can write to you here on an old school desk, the kind that is desktop and chair in one. There is a vending machine Chatty swears is the same one whose lineup the girls used to memorize when they were snowed in and bored. She said nobody ever ate the Good 'n' Plentys because that is what they called the Trustees, the monied donors of laboratory and pool.

There is a television in here now. I'll watch whatever is on, such as the swimsuit special that I watched with Warren. It was actually about the *making* of the special, and it intercut footage of the models arching their backs in the surf with segments in which the photographer described what he had had to do to get that shot. Warren became irritated by the photographer's intrusion. He said it was like being a teenager and trying to masturbate to *Petticoat Junction,* moaning, "Betty Jo, Billie Jo, Bobbie Jo . . ." and all of a sudden there's—*Uncle* Joe!

My watching whatever Warren is watching is over-compensation for Chatty telling Warren what I said about his habits—that he watches too much, and what he watches is dumb. I have done this all my life, insisting, when caught out, that, "I *do* want to be your partner, and I *like* your ideas, and let's do *many more* projects together." Karen calls this syndrome "Tour of the Lodge." Her family bought an old fishing lodge on a scenic lake in Maine. It had been shut down for many years before they cleaned the place up and moved in. Karen said she would be riding her bike in the nearby hills and meet people on vacation who would stop their cars and ask her if the old fishing lodge was still open. No, Karen would say, the place has been shut down for years. And the disappointed travelers would begin to reminisce about the happy times there when the family was together, and Karen would wind up saying, The truth is *we* bought the fishing lodge, and if you've got the time, why don't you come on over and take a walk through. And then forfeit half a day to give nostalgic strangers a tour of the lodge.

I have left this place only one other time, to go into town with Chatty. She took me into the jewelry store—accessories. I usually wear silver (I did the day we met, you might recall), but the earrings Chatty was urging me to buy were gold domes embedded with small fake jewels.

"They look like a gift from someone who likes me but doesn't know me very well," I said.

"Like when you see men in pink sweaters," Chatty said.

I turned the counter mirror, put the earrings on, hooked my hair behind my ears.

"What would I wear them with?" I asked Chatty. "They don't go with anything I own."

"Then you'll have to start life anew," Chatty said.

I think you would like Chatty, though she can be a strong cup of tea. She has hit the change of life, and told me about a niece's wedding where she had to step back from the carved-ice swan—she thought she was going to melt it. She is given to asking leading questions ("How

many feet do *you* use when you drive?") and making pro-
nouncements with which you cannot argue: "I would
rather buy a lot of presents for ten dollars each than a few
for a hundred dollars that *look* like they cost ten."

I am the only one who seems to like her jokes. She
tells them wrong, and I think her way is better. The one
about Christa McAuliffe and Donna Rice both going
down on the *Challenger?* Chatty told it this way: They
both had sex all over Florida.

Chatty is surprised I like her. She says women who
have only met her in line at a movie don't like her. She
says she had always acted as if she were God's Gift, and
then it had turned out—she *was* God's Gift.

Chatty seems content here. She says what is there to
rush home to except threatening stacks of third-class
mail.

Chatty believes in poltergeists, and I am the only person here who does, too. I believe in it all. Can I tell you
about London?—how outside of London, in a manor
house run by the National Trust, I saw the ghost of a girl
throw the ghost of a ball in an orchard for her little ghost
dog? The girl was skipping soundlessly; the dog's jaws
worked but there was no bark to hear. I saw them
through an upstairs window, on the pane of which was
scratched the date the mistress of the house had jumped.
The date was the 1600s, and I knew to look for it from
the guidebook to the house. The book said nothing about
a ghost girl and dog.

The hair did not rise on my arms beneath my coat. The ghosts were a bonus and a comfort on the third and final stop of the tour I was on. I had lagged behind the group that had gone on ahead to look at ebonized, gilded armchairs in a dead duke's bedchamber.

We had stopped first at a cathedral whose famous spire was hidden under a tower of scaffold. The cathedral's famous choir was in concert in another country, so I bought tapes of their anthems and an evensong service, and breathed musty incense as the hour was marked by carillon. Grazing nearby were sheep descended from those whose wool, the sale of it, had built the cathedral. There were cows in the fields, too. I had just learned what the ancients used for shovels, that the trenches surrounding the site were dug from chalk with the shoulder blades of cattle.

The guidebook said that the mistress of the house had scratched the date in the window with the diamond in her ring. This is something I have always wanted to do—scratch on glass with a diamond.

A heavy fog had opened and then filled itself in. I wanted to stay at the window of that house, and never mind the veneered pianofortes and the lacquered candlestands. The girl and her dog were still visible below, keeping to the gravel path inside the court, then pausing for the girl to sit and rest on a weathered goblin-carved bench.

I watched until the girl stood up and led her dog, a kind of spaniel, to the South Gate of the garden. I could see, on the overthrow, the family coat of arms, and then the girl and her dog were gone. I looked up the gardens in the guidebook. There was a view from the South Gate of the formal avenues, the labyrinth of boxwood and yew. Close up, I could see the family motto as well as their coat of arms; translated from the Latin: No man can harm me unpunished.

The girl had not seemed to see me watching, although maybe ghosts know? Without having to turn to look up at you? These ghosts were not the first ghosts I had seen, but they were the first ones I saw that moved, as when the girl, who was dressed in a long white pinafore and short leather lace-up boots, threw the ball and her spaniel dog let it bounce on the ground before he jumped up to catch it in the air.

The ghosts I had seen before were at Stonehenge. They were the ghosts of roads—the long pairs of parallel lines leading up to the site, barely visible in the sod of surrounding fields. The roads of prehistory—dents now like the tracks a vacuum cleaner leaves in thick carpet. They made me think of American baseball fields and of the men who mow them daily, criss-crossing the green in different patterns every day, and of how—if the home team won—the men would repeat the pattern they had mowed the winning day.

On the bus on the way to our third and final stop, there was the cicada sound of automatic cameras on rewind.

And then the ghosts. And the stopped clocks. Stopped at the moment the duke had died.

The watch I lost the day we met was a cheap watch with twelve dots of radium green for the numbers, but with none of the stuff painted on the hands. Knowing this did not keep me from looking in the dark at my arm, where what I could see was my watch but not the time.

I'm glad for the poltergeist here, the one that unscrews lightbulbs in the lamps, that leaves them loose in their sockets.

One day I asked the gardener what had gone wrong with my tulips. The last time I planted tulips (I am going back years here), they had bloomed right out of the ground—they had bloomed without stems, and had looked like ground cover. The gardener said the problem was low self-esteem. Then he laughed at my expression and said the bulbs had been confused, they must not have been planted deep enough and so had gotten warm, then cold, then warm again, until finally, confused, they had given up and bloomed.

I didn't tell the gardener that I had planted them half as deep as recommended to save them the work of pushing up through all that dirt. It seems that there is a lesson here, staring me in the face. I told you about the tulips to tell you something ordinary. The way, watching a movie, you find you want to scream, "Doesn't anyone eat or sleep in this film?"

All I remember of church when I was a child is a part of a sermon about the ordinary. The title of the sermon was "The Blessing of Dailiness," and had to do with why we should thank God for our toothbrush in the morning. We should thank God that each day must begin with an ordinary ritual, and not go immediately into crisis. It's a time-honored fact that after a close call, we all embrace the ordinary. But that is because it has become miraculous. Or *we* have—alive to see it.

In England, in another century, the "ordinary" was a clergyman appointed to prepare criminals for the death penalty. The clergyman would wind up his day in a house whose every fixture and appointment sprang from, and paid homage to, a politer way of living. How did he prepare them, the criminals, do you think?

You know, I often feel the effect of a place only after I leave it.

England!

Outside of London, a surprise I got was: the site was roped off. You had to view the site like an exhibit in a museum. It made me give up to learn that until a few years ago, you could hire a man in the village to chip off pieces of Stonehenge for you, to keep as souvenirs.

The guide gave us twenty minutes. Those of us on the tour found out that you cannot walk the circumference of the site and return to the bus in twenty minutes.

You could walk the roped path, mud through the sheep-cropped grass, until the anxiety of being late and missing the bus turned you back around. At a point on the path, I held out my arm and cupped my hand so that it looked as though I was holding the site in my hand.

The highway you drive in on is very close to the monument. It is possible to pull over onto the shoulder and lean out a window and take a picture without leaving the car. I watched people do that. It was jarring, like finding the rope-laden stanchions holding us back.

I have seen things my mother never saw.

I often feel the effects of people only after they leave me.

In a locked metal box I took when my mother died, there is a button she would pin to her jacket on the days she led tours as a docent at the museum. "Art Has Drawing Power"—she never got tired of it.

My mother took me to the art museum once on a day she worked as a guide. I followed her on her rounds; it was a sunny day when few people wanted to be inside. I tagged along with a couple of stragglers who insisted they be given a tour.

Her remarks that day were perfunctory. I suspected her of cutting back the usual presentation. And then it became obvious. Who was there for her to impress? She showed us into the Seventeenth-Century Gallery. She motioned toward the portraits mounted on darkened walls, and said, "Dutch. Seventeenth century."

She was going to lead us into another wing!

But I had studied in secret to surprise her. I got the attention of the visitors, and before my mother could usher them out, I offered up the history of Protestant Baroque. How I loved what I had memorized—with neither Catholic churches to embellish with religious images, nor a court to foot the bill for grandiose art, with the Calvinist edict not to corrupt God's majesty with fantasy, "So it was to the objects in the world around him that the Dutch painter turned," I intoned.

Apple-polishing toady.

"You're in my way," my mother said through her teeth when I came to the end of my speech.

The button I wore at the time said, "You Look the Part."

Warren rides a bike to the dining hall wearing a T-shirt that has printed on it, "One Less Car." He got it in town at the place whose best-selling T-shirt in summer says, "So Many Tourists, So Few Bullets." Tourists are the ones who invariably snap them up.

Summer slows us down. Does it slow you down, too? I like to close a book I've been reading on the porch and picture you swimming in your backyard pool. I see you swimming alone, with no one waiting to wrap you in a robe when you climb out. This letter is a robe I hold out to you.

The article didn't say if you swam before or after you work. Wouldn't the chlorine bother you if you swam before you painted? But maybe you have that new filtration system, the one that uses ions. I don't feel like I've been in a pool unless I come out with eyes red and stinging.

I told you I never had a pool, but that gives the wrong impression. My best friend was a champion swimmer. We wanted to be wet, and every weekday we were. Even after a shower, our skin smelled chlorinated. With a strainer on the end of a stick, we would flip the turtles, moles, and frogs from out of our neighbors' pools. The builder of these pools had since gone out of business, and no longer honored his service contracts. Sometimes we would have missed a frog from the time before. Trapped in the filter, floating in chlorine, the frog would bleach out white. Green or white, the frogs' eyes were open as we sailed them over fences into other people's yards.

Warren caught me on the porch with a catalog of your work. He leaned over my shoulder and said, "What does he get for a painting like that?"

I didn't answer, and he practiced the trick he swears he can do where you flex your arm when a mosquito lights on it so the mosquito can't detach itself until the sheer force of your blood pressure makes the mosquito explode. He has not succeeded yet, though earlier I saw him rid Little Egypt of a hornet, luring it out with a dead fly placed on the offered straw of a broom. When proud of himself, he chants tongue twisters for us. He made up

"Shoes and socks shock Chatty." Sometimes when I pass his door at night, I can hear from behind it the rapid refrains of "sifted thistles" and "mixed biscuits."

Last night I was in the library waiting to go in to dinner. I shifted my legs away from Warren, and snagged my stockings on the wicker chair. As though it had been his fault, I shot Warren a sour look, so he went on to dinner without me. I opened the book in whose margins he had scribbled, "How foolish we were to fear loneliness!" and next to a particularly Latinate passage, "Oh, get off your stilts."

Dinner was one of those times when the past gets a good going-over. Chatty and Warren and Karen all have access to their pasts. Does it matter that I can't remember if the living room couch I built a fort behind was black or tweed or plaid? Or if something I think I did turns out to be in *Jane Eyre?* So much of the time, what I came away with from a day was the shape of my mother's barrette, and not what she said to me. They were always made of tortoise shell; some of them were oval, some were square. The barrettes were large, and held a low ponytail. It is the easiest way to keep hair out of your face, but I won't do it—it makes me look too much like her. Warren has a heart-shaped island, and I have a heart-shaped face. Karen has the face I would want if I could choose, but maybe you would say that the unconventional face is the one you would rather paint? Forget about her—just keep thinking about me.

Didn't you think it was odd to find raisins in your "fresh" fruit salad?

When I was in school, I often got sick from the fear of classes. I fought off the feeling by keeping a fistful of raisins with me. Before going into a class, I would shake part of a box of raisins into my hand, and close my fingers tight around them. Steadily, throughout the hour of class, I would take a single raisin—now warm and plump with sweat—and slip it into my mouth when the teacher couldn't see. I never chewed the raisins. I would swallow each one as a hedge against the nausea, and so get through each class. I needed the most raisins in math, the fewest in English. I kept this up until I finished junior high, just as, years later, I swallowed pills, tranquilizers, to get me through a day, no longer staving off nausea but a feeling of approaching doom. For me, raisins are still so completely pharmacological that I'm surprised when I see them in grocery stores, in cellophane-wrapped "lunchbox" packages of six.

I can't stand raisins now, and was relieved when you separated them and left them on your plate. As you might imagine, folks here take exception to what is on their plates, too. My first night here, Chatty warned me away from the fruit drinks, concocted as they are in the blender the gardener used once to whip up a frothy pitcher of mole repellant—equal parts cod liver oil and dish-washing detergent—which he painted along the rodents' corded trails in the garden.

Despite Chatty's success with the long-gone Centennial Garden, she says she can't bring herself to spend any time in this one. Warren said, "It could be argued that you do not get the full measure of the experience here if you don't take advantage of the garden," and Chatty told him, "*We're* what's going on here, so by having dinner with you, I'm taking in the attractions." She took a small pouch out of the pocket of her smock and emptied it onto the tablecloth. "Coquilles sucre," she said, sliding one at a time across the cloth to my place with her finger. Sugar shells, hard as rocks, in scuffed colors of coral, white and blue, like pieces of sea glass, their shine tumbled off in salt water.

"One of the attendants gets them for me in town," Chatty said.

Other people bring their own food to the table, as long as it has been approved ahead of time. Chatty told me a woman had gagged when she tried to swallow but instead inhaled a dry spoonful of Spirulina, a faddish powdered supplement that was meant to be stirred in fruit juice and would turn it an evil green.

Karen swallows Gore Vidal. Then she swallows Donald Trump. She takes a blue capsule and a gold spansule—a B-complex and an E—and puts them on the tablecloth a few inches apart. She points the one at the other. "Martha Stewart," she says, "meet Oprah Winfrey." She swallows them both without water.

My first night, unsolicited, Warren leaned across the table and confided, "The way to keep an ice-cream cone from dripping on your shirt? Before you put ice cream into one of those pointed cones, put in a miniature marshmallow to plug up any leaks. You can eat it at the end," he pointed out.

I don't really care what is on the table, as long as it isn't raisins. Tonight we ordered in pizza, and the pizza-with-everything looked like a bad neighborhood. It is after dinner that I think about home. Across the way there are beer bottles lined up alongside the grave of the young man whose motorcycle stalled on the tracks. Not empties, but full bottles of Budweiser, capped. The malevolent twins steal in and drink them warm, hiding behind a towering hedge that encircles a trio of well-tended graves—the doctor who took two wives, sisters. The twins drink their bottles of stolen beer and think no one hears them snorting at dusk, then they put on wigs—black Afros from the sixties—and pretend to have sex in the hammock back of their house.

A woman on horseback walks the gravel paths. She is someone the twins have spied on, watching from the woods as she mucked stalls dressed in a string bikini, muttering "Perverts" at the yardmen who stared. In summer, in the cemetery, she climbs down and clips the white French lilacs that grow in one spot, spliced by rotting cedar. In the fall, she helps herself to dried hydrangea clusters, voluptuous, no doubt, on her dining room table. Her horse lifts its tail, and unleashed dogs escape nearby yards to come and feast, snapping, the way they scramble for clippings from hooves in her stable.

High winds redistribute bouquets, and Alice Parker's roses blow to Grace Hall one row over; carnations intended for Henry Hand work loose from a vase and are trapped by the stone of Red Howell, Senior, interred at Indianapolis.

At dinner this evening, Warren talked about his pet. He said he had had a spider monkey named Elmer and Chatty interrupted, having heard it as "monkey spider," to tell the table about the one she and her ex-husband had seen (from where they lay beneath mosquito netting covering their bed) climb into a wardrobe in their rented villa in Nevis.

"We left the island without our clothes," Chatty said.

Warren continued. "My parents rented a place in Hatteras where we were supposed to spend the summer. Me and my sister and our parents and Elmer and about a million crazed mosquitoes. My dad read where you could order chameleons through the mail, so he bought two dozen of them, and let them loose in the house. My mother called it a harmonious solution, until we got home from the beach the next day and Elmer met us at the top of the stairs with what turned out to be the last two chameleons, one in each fist. When he saw us," Warren said, "he waved them over his head like pennants. When my mother screamed at him, Elmer brought one fist to his mouth and bit the head off the chameleon. Then he did the same thing with the other."

I asked him if monkeys know right from wrong, and Warren said, "Elmer was a goblin from hell. He used to jump on the dogs' backs and make them carry him around the house until they learned to duck under the coffee table and knock the bastard off."

Warren burned himself putting out a cigarette, and Karen began to cry. Warren took a long drink from his Coke can.

"Thought you quit," Chatty said.

Chatty looked beneficently around the table. "I am getting better," she said. "So the others are starting to fail."

That time I was in London, I went to an elegant dinner for which the chef assembled a roast turkey inside of which was lodged a goose, inside of which was a duck that housed a chicken that contained a game hen—all of them boned and served with a dark, tart currant sauce. I think of that dinner, of the chef slicing through the five fowl, when I imagine what kind of woman you like. A woman who contains a series of surprises? There are clues in the women you have had, though the thought of ask-

ing you what you like is like the team of artists who hired
a marketing firm to find out what Americans want in a
painting. The artists painted the result of the poll which
found that what we want is a blue painting the size of a
dishwasher with a biblical figure and landscape.

I am so suggestible. When Chatty asks if I am hungry, I say, "I could be." I would try to become the woman
you wanted without even knowing I was trying. As it is,
I am barely the woman I am.

And what if you don't like the person you are? Where
do you find the parts to make yourself into some other
kind of person? Can it be something you read in a book,
a gesture you see on the street? Half-smile of a teacher,
the walk of a girl on the beach.

I would like to go to a matinee with you. Any afternoon, any theatre, I would not care what we saw. I would
like to sit next to you in the dark in a public place and lean
over from time to time to better hear your caustic asides.

I want to ask the questions I failed to ask that day
when all I could think was: he is sitting across the table
from me, and he has ordered fruit salad! I was like the
woman who met Anaïs Nin and walked with her in Central Park, and couldn't help exclaiming that Anaïs Nin
was eating a hot dog. The woman's incredulity bothered
Anaïs Nin, just as I am sure my behavior bothered you.
But surely you are used to it.

I want to know everything about you. So I tell you
everything about myself.

A psychic once told me that I was too honest. It was the first thing he said to me before he had turned over palm or card. He was not urging duplicity; I think he meant for me to be what a certain kind of woman calls "clever."

The psychic was right, yet I am such a fraud:

"Are your parents still alive?"

"My father lives out West."

"And your mother?"

"My mother is dead."

"Of what?"

"She did it herself," I said, and let you think that that was hard on a girl, a tragedy.

Is this where I exhibited a ruinous lapse of judgment? Asking if you had known my mother when you were both in art school? You might have known each other. Yet is this an instance where I might instead have been clever, and not pointed out how much older than me you are? Worse, did you think I was suggesting that you knew my mother *well?* That maybe she posed for you?

The truth is, it was hard on me. Not her death—her life. The only surprise when she killed herself was that she had killed *herself.* I said to my father, "I always thought if she killed anyone, the one she killed would be me." And my father said, "I know."

My only job was not to get killed. At home, at school, at the movies, at a party, riding a horse, rowing a boat, skating on ice, raking the gravel drive, getting the mail, swimming in a lake, hiking in the mountains, on a bike, in a tent, in a church, in a car, eating breakfast, lunch and dinner, on Halloween, Christmas and Easter, awake and asleep, I had no other job.

Two slips of the tongue: I said to Chatty, "In all important ways, I believe I am her evil," instead of "equal." And when Chatty voiced an opinion, I added, "I feel the shame."

She has been dead twenty years, and listen to what happened to me on the street. Of all the things I could have said to the woman on the sidewalk, the woman I had never seen before, the woman who, unprovoked, had made a fist and brought it down on the side of my face, what I had said was, "Get out of me!" As though the demon was not an overweight woman in an out-of-season straw hat who had said as she swung her fist at me, "*This* is what you want!"

The other day I was playing Scrabble with Karen. I saw that I could close the space in D-E- -Y. I had an N and an F. Which do you think I chose? What was the word I made?

Sometimes, in the kitchenette here, I open a French cookbook so as not to think about her. Better to try to find out, what is a pomelo? Where could one find lemon-grass to crush with a mallet for eggplant?

Before I came here, I asked my father a question and gave him a year to answer. The question I asked him is: What is it about me that most resembles my mother?

And I will wonder during this year that follows, did I do the right thing? What will come of it? Will I get something valuable to have? And know that he will make something up, most likely, to give his daughter a gift. And in the year of waiting I will answer the question for him. The way you are most like your mother? You play tricks on people's minds. You are unlovable. I see in your eyes the love of death.

I'll give you one year, I said.

Have you detected a curious lack of medical authority here? It is only missing from my letter. There are counselors for us, wise and complex people who do not intrude but are always available—why have I not written about them sooner? They are one of the consolations, here in the present. They live in a separate wing of the main building, and drop in throughout the week. We can call them at night if we need to. Some are young and still in training. They follow the doctor, and are courteous and kind. They take it as an article of faith that bad things that happen are "occasions for transformation," that creating distance from them is different from denying they were bad.

They are not averse to joining us in games. One time we all played charades. We were uniformly bad at the game. I pulled a hard one that no one could guess, no one came close to this person's name. In a private session several days later, when my counselor asked if I had any questions, I said yes—"How would *you* have done 'Nancy Reagan'?"

At the same time each evening, a counselor checks to see that no one is going out. What he asks us sounds like, "Urine for the night?"

One night last week we had a bad moment. One of the guests—she's new—has the same name as a well-known actress. Chatty began to tell a story about the actress and as soon as she said the woman's name, she glanced at the one in the Hostility Suite with us and said, "I mean the *real* Anne Bancroft."

Our Anne Bancroft is not so crazy she didn't recognize an insult. She sat up straight in her lounger, and then she left the room.

That is not a bad way to handle an insult if you don't have a ready comeback. I learned my lesson in a foreign country. I was visiting a friend in Paris. We were riding to the Louvre in a cab. I insisted my friend let me handle the transaction, though I knew I didn't know enough French. By accident I undertipped the driver. He turned on me, an American *touriste*. I recognized the word *putain*—the driver had called me a whore. I remember that I tried for a French *hauteur,* and said, "Je *suis, suis*-je!" I realized that what I was saying was English with French clothes on, and slunk away in defeat. (A saleswoman at a pet store later neutralized the cabbie. I went to a fancy shop on the Rue de Trop Cher to buy a friend's dog a collar. The saleswoman, before she would show me the collars, asked, "What kind of dog is he?" I said, "He's a beagle," and the saleswoman said, "No, no—I mean, what's he like?")

The first time I walked one of the nearby shelter dogs, I broke into futile tears. I said to one of the counselors, "There are twelve million others in this country alone that I am not able to help!" And she said, "It doesn't have to be complete, your help. The goal is not to erase the problem. You do it to make the choice, to give and get joy in this life."

And I said to her, still in tears, "But it is not enough!" And then I asked her, "What is enough? Enough energy, attention, effort, et cetera." She said, "The answer lies in the practice. In balance with what comes naturally." I said, "How can I, a six, help anyone else until I am better?" And she said, "Helping someone else can *make* you better."

In large part, we are meant to heal each other. The garden is a metaphor. Seeding, tending, weeding, watering—all leading up to the harvest. Although leave it to Warren to point out these words that are synonymous with "plant": hide, secrete, conceal, bury, entomb.

Warren says, of the place he was before this, "My counselor was a moron, and he helped me."

There is one counselor here we suspect of being something more. She gives such encouraging and optimistic guidance that one day I asked if I could tape her. We set a time to meet for a talk on the patio off the parlor. I turned on my pocket-sized tape recorder and showed her where to speak into the mike. She delivered a kind of pep talk, one I could now replay and refer to as the need arose.

The need arose the very next day, so I grabbed my tape recorder, fitted in her tape, and went up to deserted Little Egypt. I pressed the "On" button, and closed my eyes. I let myself believe her good words; they displaced my bad thoughts for the length of an hour. When it was over, I pressed the "Off" button. Nothing happened. The tape continued to wind in its cartridge. I held the "Off" button down with my thumb, and still the tape played, though there was no more voice to hear. I ran downstairs with it, found Warren in the Hostility Suite. I handed him the tape recorder, said, "Can you turn this off for me?" Warren was not able to turn the machine off until he had smacked the recorder into his palm and then against the table edge to empty the batteries out.

Not graduating is how Chatty left this place the first time. This time, all she will have to do is call a car, just as I have done. I have learned to specify *town car* so the company does not send over a limousine. I remember to tell them to tell the driver to bring along something to read.

With my bags packed and in the car with me, it is like the concert I went to—a chamber quartet—at what was once a private home, a Victorian mansion. In the music room there was a birdcage that had finches in it. The cage was a replica of the house it was inside of, down to the mansard roof and broad-stepped porch. That night I arrived early and heard the musicians already playing. Thinking my watch was slow and I was actually late, I hurried in. The musicians were playing—not tuning up, but performing the evening's program—to an empty house. And the finches were singing along! When they finished, the cellist explained to me that before every concert given in the house, the musicians played first for the finches so the birds would tire themselves out singing, and would then remain quiet during the concert that was scheduled.

Chatty assures me I will know, I will "just know" when to leave. How does she come by such certainty?

Who said sanity is free? *That* is the answer to Karen's complaint about always having to do two jobs.

Don't you find that there is no right place to begin? When you try to make sense of a thing that has happened? That everything is as important, or as unimportant, as everything else? A poet writes, "He opens a book at random, and consults randomness." To me, this is what it seems. To me and, Warren has pointed out, a million other people.

I pretend I know you well. I say to Warren, "I have a friend who—" and Warren says, "You have too many friends."

I waited so long to write to you. I liked knowing, as it came to me throughout the course of a day, that I would be writing a letter to you. It made me think of a doctor here, a man who said he'd have liked to have treated Marilyn Monroe, what a lift it would have given him to look in his appointment book and see her name. He had lifted up for a moment on the toes of his shoes.

Warren taped a one-word sign to his wall. The word that he wakes to is: Headlong. Writing to you, it is my word, too. And, hey—here's hoping you like blue! This is the color my mother used to use, though she chose the stock with a ragged edge, and I prefer my edges sharp. She fit what she had to say on a thank-you note.

The pond is surrounded by winter-stripped trees, packed so close together the lack of leaves doesn't matter. There is no seeing through them to the single man and woman who proceed across the cracked black ice on borrowed skates. No crack of the puck. No Rock 'n' Skate, no Rap 'n' Skate, no programmed medleys threatening disco. The sound of speed on blades. Turtles float below. We are humming "The Nutcracker Suite."

My consolations are many, their power no less for not including you. I said to a psychic just after our tea, "There is a person I met," and the psychic cut me off, saying, "He is a thief. He will steal your soul."

The man ran groups. He took a token fee from people wanting to quit—smoking, drinking, eating too much. "Picture the thing you want to live without." "My husband," one woman whispered to another. I shut my eyes with the rest of them and tried to conjure fear, what I want to live without.

The counselors here say we often mistake excitement for apprehension, for fear. They say it is up to us, that we can forcibly jog ourselves from one state into the other. But it sounds to me like my favorite joke when I was a girl: What is Pollyanna's epitaph? "I'm *glad* I'm dead."

The psychic said I would have two children. This makes me shake my head. I know you are not supposed to leave a baby alone. Not even for a minute. But after a while I think, What could happen to a baby in the time it would take for me to run to the corner for a cappucino to go? So I do it, I run to the corner and get the cappucino. And then think how close the store is that is having the sale on leather gloves. Really, I think, it is only a couple of blocks. So I go to the store and I buy the gloves. And it hits me—how long it has been since I have gone to a movie. A matinee! So I do that, too. I go to a movie. And when I come out of the theatre, it occurs to me that it has been years since I have been to Paris. Years. So I go to Paris, and come back three months later and find a skeleton in the crib.

No one has ever told me that I am good with children. Shortly before I came here I went to a dinner party. The hostess was setting the table—there were eight of us that night—when her daughter, a barefoot seven-year-old, demanded we play the game.

I had not played the game before. You had to build a tower out of narrow cross-placed pieces of wood, then pull away the pieces one at a time without making the tower collapse.

I am not good at games, and the girl was sure of her moves. Yet somehow I was good at this, and when the girl removed the piece that made the tower fall, she ran to her mother screaming, "I didn't lose!"

The mother put the child to bed and lay beside the child for a while in the bed.

When I go to sleep, I sleep on the side of the bed my mother used to sleep on. Sometimes, at dawn, I wake up and find myself in the pose my mother died in—lying on her side, her arm reaching from under her head as though she were doing the sidestroke in a pool, the pills she had swallowed weighing her down like so many pebbles in her pockets.

I don't fall asleep with my body on the bed in the same way my mother was found. It must be a thing I go into when I am asleep. And still I cannot be sure that, limb for limb, I am in the same position. My mother's legs, when I saw her, were covered by the sheet; it is possible that my legs are bent where my mother's legs were straight.

Sometimes it feels as though I won't be able to live until I can sleep in a position of my own—not in the way my mother's body was found on the bed, but in a way that is mine—even if it is only a sort of dead man's float where you don't use a muscle but clasp both your knees and let your head sink into the pillow, rocking gently as a baby, tipping your head to the side to take in air, conserving your strength until help arrives, or until you can save yourself, there in bed.

Consolation is a beautiful word. *Everyone* skins his knee—that doesn't make yours hurt any less. The standard line here.

Karen's consolation is a dog. Mine, too, some of the time. In the lobby of the shelter you can buy a bag of biscuits and pass them out through the kennel bars while an attendant readies a dog for you to walk. Last time I went I collected the loose fur from the dogs just groomed to make a present to the gardener to stuff guess where. Then I walked Shauna. She is a young shepherd mix who had a litter of ten that had to be weaned early, at the age of five weeks, because the mother developed mastitis from nursing so many.

The attendant handed me Shauna's leash, and Shauna leaped into the air. Her belly sagged, and was covered with long scabs, but once outside she ran for a mile, pulling me along at the end of a leash. When I finally had to rest, I said, "Shauna, shhh," and she sat down and leaned against my leg, waiting.

When I brought her back to the shelter, I went to see

her puppies in a private room. They were no more than eight inches long. I sat on the floor and they moved as a single mass onto me. They were crying and mewing like kittens. They licked and bit and tried to suck as they moved up my arms and chest, clinging to my neck and reaching up to bat at my face and nose, around my ears.

Once I walked Shauna in a nearby park where a group of people holding leads stood huddled in conversation while their dogs, off-leash, played close by. Shauna and I stood at the edge of both groups, and I heard a woman brag, "Barney makes on command." Another woman observed her dog as it was mounted by two others in succession; she said that her dog's social life was better than her own.

I was watching TV in Little Egypt with Chatty when a dog food commercial came on. A litter of tumbling pups crossed the screen, and Chatty said to me, "I guess *you're* happy."

I've never heard it said of you that you had dogs as pets. Though surely when you were a boy, a boy on a working farm, there must have been a dog that you befriended?

Do you find consolation in a person? In a woman? I found it once with a man, but I lost my combs. This was the last time I saw him. In the cab going home is when I saw the combs, one on top of the other on the table beside his couch. It would have been better if he had been the one to remove them, but when they interfered with the travel of his hands, I was the one who reached up and slipped the combs out. They are just cheap plastic, their job not to ornament but to secure and vanish in hair. It is not like leaving behind an earring, something that needs to be joined with a mate. The combs cost nothing, so he did not think to return them. But they're the only ones that work in my kind of hair, and you can't often find the ones that blend in with your hair. They tend to be packaged in assortments of a dozen, in garish bright primary colors. Before I left that night, I used his hairbrush when we finished. I left long hairs caught in the bristles, making of his hairbrush a kind of reliquary.

Where is the consolation in this? It is in humiliation, which brings the softness of heart that allows you to listen to God.

"You a student over at the college?" The cabdriver, gunning for a tip.

I still want those combs back. I need all the things I left behind back. Better to find consolation in a place. At the beach. A day at the beach when everything rhymes: crabs picked clean, one thong—green, flies blown in on a warm land breeze, parking lot rainbow in a pool of gasoline; diving seagulls, blasted boat hulls, sea-scarred plastic, rusted bedstead, rotting refuse, fish now dead.

Sometimes I worry that we don't talk about ideas. But Warren says, "I hate ideas," and Chatty says, "Ideas, sugar, are not sexy."

So a lot of the time it's moisturizers and accessories, physical fitness and hair. And still so many ways to go wrong, as when I said to Chatty, hadn't she colored her hair, and Chatty's frosty reply, that she had not *colored* her hair, she had *enhanced* it.

We talk about clothes. On the theory that generic elements improve with repetition, Chatty wears two identical cashmere sweaters, layered one over the other. My own closet, an ugly-dress bonanza, yields sacklike black washed silk. Chatty can wear what she likes; she eats two desserts a night and you would never know it. Whereas the rest of us would gain weight even if we had food poisoning.

Karen presents herself in tooth-torn shirts. She showed up in the Hostility Suite with a miniature dachshund from the shelter. She held the dog in her lap, and while Chatty went on at some length about the plans she had for her wardrobe, Karen ran her opal ring down over the dog's ears—ears she had made stand up like a rabbit's—the way you thread the ends of a silk scarf through a scarf ring. Karen said that she had had this kind of dog when she was just out of college, and had taken the dog to restaurants where she would wipe out an ashtray with her napkin, and crumble part of a hamburger into it for her dog. She said she would get her dog's leash and ask the dog —not, Want to go for a walk? but, Want to go out to lunch?

Chatty told Karen that one thing's for sure—when

you have a child, your dog becomes a pet. That would not happen to me. I can't stand the sound of a person eating, but I love the sound of a dog crunching down on kibble. I love a dog's appetite. The appetite of a baby is a frightening thing to me. I watch a mother spoon food into her baby's mouth, then spoon back in what the baby spits out; to me, it is the job of spackling. If I had a baby, I would change overnight from a woman who worries about the calories in the glue of an envelope to someone who goes to the corner for coffee, a nightgown showing beneath my coat, the hem of that gown clawed to shreds by a cat.

My mother gave away my dogs; when she died, she died with cats. A calico cat sat tucked like a hen on her chest, as though it were hatching her death. A Siamese cat, when my mother was gone, yowled in her empty room.

I don't know that I have ever seen a cat in one of your paintings. Or a dog. All those paintings, portraits of friends, and not one friend that was dog. *My* first friend was a Labrador retriever. His name was Needles, and I would saddle him up with a folded bath towel held on with my father's belt. Needles obeyed only one command in the house. He would run into the living room and you would have to call out, "Swerve!"—one of us would have to call it out—and he *would* swerve just before he would have crashed into the glass-topped table.

My mother gave him away.

I was at school. When I came home, there was on my desk a dimestore turtle swimming the shallow moat around a ramped plastic island—island of the plastic palm—in search of specks of lettuce.

Surely it is in part the medication, but we have hung our libidos on hooks outside the door. Do men play a version of the game women do, when a woman asks herself in, say, a shopping center, If I had to go to bed with someone in this store, which one would it be? Here, Warren is the best of the lot. If I can return to the high school mixer, a girl would go up to another girl and say of one of the boys, "He's really cute." And suddenly the girl to whom this was said, a girl who had not previously noticed this fellow, was taking another look and thinking to herself, "He *is* really cute."

Where was I going with this? I mean to say that if Chatty said such a thing to me, I still wouldn't see it, given a push.

That gorilla I met, the one who signs, was given a push, but it didn't work. The people with whom she lives wanted her to mate. They brought in a suitable male, younger and larger than she, and set them up to cohabit. The female gorilla signed to him things like, "Hurry up," (and give her more bananas), and "Truck not yours," (a Tonka Toy truck). Neither gorilla would make a move, so the people rented an X-rated film and screened it for the primates. It held the gorillas' attention, and when the film was over, the female gorilla signed to the male, "Climb up my back." But he did not have her language skills, and did not otherwise take the hint.

My libido, what is left of it, flows in your direction. By the time I recognized you in the bookstore and boldly asked if I could buy you a cup of coffee, I had already constructed you in my mind, even though a voice in my head cried out: Don't confuse the painting with the painter— let's not forget the example of Picasso!

Given the hours I think of you, given the hours in my white-sheeted bed, you would think I could cook up a scene or two. But I can picture nothing that has not already happened. And so I am stuck with: a cup of tea in a public place on a winter afternoon. A failure of imagination? Or a self-protecting check, a screen blacked out when the home team plays.

Except I let myself imagine that you are painting my portrait. I offered myself as model to a teacher when I was a teen (having just read *The Prime of Miss Jean Brodie*). I worked up my nerve to do this—didn't he sometimes paint nudes? But he painted me fully clothed. He painted me looking out a window, looking away. Yearning? The painter had just quit drinking. *I* was not what he was interested in.

When you paint me, I sit in a darkened room. I lean toward a dark desk, quill pen in my hand. I am dressed in a fur-trimmed yellow satin mantle; my hair is beribboned and pulled back from my face. Does this sound familiar? Are you with me on this? "Woman Writing a Letter," by Vermeer.

Look at me. My concerns—are they spiritual, do you think, or carnal? Come on. We've read our Shakespeare. "There's no art/To find the mind's construction in the face."

And what are my chances of enacting "Young Woman Reading a Letter at an Open Window"? I have, as you can see, no wiles or guile, the things I would need to elicit a letter from you in return. I would change this if I could, this curse of earnestness. Am I out of my mind?—putting my cards on the table! A woman should conceal, not reveal. Now my lipstick is chewed off, my lingerie is dingy, my high heels scuffed and broken.

There was reportedly a painting of a woman writing a letter that was found in Vermeer's studio at his death.

I would like to know—did you see me that day as a woman? Did you think of me just as a fan? The way you have painted women—do you see us that way in the flesh? Do you ask permission to paint someone, or does she offer herself to you? Or do you paint a woman from memory, taking her without her knowing? Are you clinical as a doctor, or do you fall in love a little? Do you start out painting one woman and end up painting another?

This is what happens to me. I start out being myself, and end up being my mother. It isn't something I try to do. In fact, I try hard not to. That is the crucial difference: I don't want to end my life, but I can't keep myself from trying.

The pills that she swallowed were mine. They were pills prescribed to me because I couldn't sleep. With as much thoughtfulness as she showed me in her life, she left one behind in the vial. Presumably, it would be hard for me to sleep the night we found her.

I have never slept better.

I saw a movie in which two girls share an apartment. One day, one of the girls opens the other's diary and makes an entry in it as though she is the diary owner. It scared me, that scene, because what—except for dying—could be scarier than merging?

Men are afraid this will happen with women. Often, after an intimate visit, a man will pick a fight. Have you done this yourself? I find you can count on it. And the closer you have been, the more snappish after. To separate himself, to keep from being pulled in. I have learned to head this off. I find an excuse to take myself away. I find this is easier all around. Even if where I take myself is into the next room, to sit and listen to music.

Do you listen to music while you work? I would if I were a painter. You know the way children ask which of your senses you would give up if you had to make a choice—your hearing or your sight? Before I saw your paintings, I would have given up my sight. It is the choice I used to make.

*   *   *

Warren and I watch reruns in Little Egypt, seventies sit-coms. A man tries to teach his friend a lesson. He says, Do you see what happens when you *assume?* You make an "ass" out of "u" and "me." But what is a life without assumptions?

Failing to engage us with clothes, Chatty makes us talk to her about men. As many men as we remember. Some, like you, have been painters. Maybe *all* of them have been painters. Even the gardener here, when he isn't numbing our minds with endless talk of bud count and petal length, will set up an easel during his break, and produce a passable landscape. He will tell us the story of the Chinese paintings in which the time of day could be ascertained by the dilation of the cat's pupils and the degree to which the peonies had opened. Happy pastime, painting. And when it is a man's work, it is work he will enjoy. Although Warren feels it isn't work if it isn't hard. "Why do you think they call it work?" he says. With no need of segue, Chatty is off on Edward, the man she says we will meet when he comes to call on her here.

"Edward is bad," Chatty says, not without pride. "But he doesn't think he is bad. He thinks I can't see things clearly."

"And you can't," Warren says.

"You think the moment he behaves untenably, you'll leave," Chatty says. "But you find yourself saying, 'He's been *so* nice until now . . .' So you think, 'I'll ignore it,' and pretty soon you're ignoring New York City. And then watch—he'll have to put *me* out the door."

"He could change." My tentative entry into the conversation.

Chatty looks at me as though she does not know where to begin. She says that instances of change are anecdotal, deep-seated fantasy. "The New Testament has versions of it over and over: the whore becomes a saint, Paul on the road to Damascus. I mean," she says, "Christianity acknowledges that for a person to change his nature is *miraculous.*"

"It's not as if *we* change, either," Karen puts in.

"What I think," Chatty says, "is that if a man loves a woman more than a woman loves a man, then they're even. The thing to remember," Chatty says as though reminding herself, "is that a man is not obligated to love you. Once you reach that philosophical state, *he* feels your grip loosening, and *you* retain your dignity. Otherwise, you go nuts, you're subject to the dark undertow of it all."

And I say, "Can't a normal person take a walk on the dark side? If she watches where she took her last step?" Thinking of you, and thinking this is the moment when Chatty will ask, What is the *deal* with this guy? And knowing if I told her your parting words to me—"We'll see each other again"—she would look at me with pity, not giving your words the right spin.

But Chatty just passes a bowl of bitter scrotilized olives. "When I get out of here, Edward wants me to visit," she says.

"He's fixing up his house, and I'm afraid he will want me to help. He'll open a section of Sheetrock—there'll be clouds of bees and rotting honey. I call his house The Hive. I told him to hire help, but the local help is Lawrence Home Improvement—Larry and his scrap-hoarding teenaged son. Larry's motto is: Pound to Fit, Paint to Match."

"But you're good at all that," I tell her. "You know what goes with what."

"It's hopeless," Chatty says. "I'll say, Paint this trim *lobster bisque,* and I come back and they've made it *terra-cotta.*"

Which brings me back to the question, How does she come by such certainty? How does anyone? My mother, believing she could give away my dog—and she could!

And what about the certainty I feel regarding you? You could say that an hour is not a lot to go on. But always, before, a thing didn't work because I was too young and too old. Too dumb and too smart. But I learn from my mistakes. The certainty I feel—it is something to hit back with. So in a manner of speaking, I now have a stick that is bigger than the stick I was beaten with.

Except let's not think of it as something larger of the same type. Maybe, instead of a stick, it just looks like a stick. Maybe it is really a snake. And it moves like a river. Maybe it *is* a river, and we can go someplace on it, someplace new.

"You still writing that letter?" Chatty says.

*   *   *

Warren: Why do dogs roll in dead animals? (Because live ones won't let them).

Warren caught sight of a mouse in Little Egypt. He traced its path back to a nest of Raisinettes, the chocolate gone chalky in the dust beneath the couch. He told us he had caught mice as a boy, that once he skinned a trap-killed mouse and made a mouse-skin rug for his sister's dollhouse. And then he was telling us again about Elmer, about Elmer his little spider monkey, climbing to the top of their Christmas tree, pelting the family with ornaments he had pulled from their places on the branches.

"We yelled at him to stop," Warren said, "and Elmer threw them harder."

That was Elmer's last Christmas, Warren told us. Elmer caught cold on New Year's Eve. He died in Warren's arms in the car Mrs. Moore drove along icy streets to the vet. Is there an animal story that doesn't end in tears? This one. Warren said the family gathered to bury Elmer in the backyard. "The dogs came, too," Warren said. "They stood with us at the edge of Elmer's grave, and kicked in some of the dug-out dirt. They couldn't wait to see that sucker in the ground."

Chatty has been having her insights again. A fall from a horse, a blow to her head some twenty years ago, left her able to approach a stranger in the park and say, I'm sorry about your husband. How did you know? the woman would then say to Chatty.

She says she can't predict when a thing like that will happen. She says sometimes she will meet a person and know then and there how and when that person will die. She knows these things for facts, but she says she would never say as much out loud.

I have heard Warren try to get information out of her, saying, "You see any reason I shouldn't get a Harley?" I have done it, too—watched her closely as I unveil plans for next year.

I know her insights are back because of last week in Little Egypt. It was the two of us in there, Chatty dozing in the rocking chair, me reading a book about—what else?— dogs. Then Chatty sat up straight; she opened her eyes and said in a firm voice, "Get back in your body right now!"

Who are you talking to? I said.

She had a letter from a cousin days later. The cousin's husband had had a heart attack. He had flat-lined in the CCU, until to everyone's amazement he had suddenly come to life, conscious. He told the medical team that he had left his body and gone to visit his wife's cousin. The day, the time, corresponded. "I was talking to my cousin's husband," Chatty had told me that night.

Without faith or courage, I hope she would do the same for me.

I told her about the dream I had the night my last dog died. I was out of town that night, asleep in a small hotel. My dog came to me in the dream, and he said aloud, "It's time."

I didn't tell her about the night my mother died, a night I dreamlessly slept through the night in the room right next to hers. But then, my mother never slept with her head on my stomach, or licked my face awake.

"Tell you about my neighbor," Chatty said. "We all of us despised him, the way he cheated us out of water when he tapped into our lines to fill his swimming pool in summer. When he sent his children over to collect for a cause, it seemed to us unlikely that the money his children collected ever left his house. He ran for the school board to keep blacks out of the schools, and sold faulty garden equipment to a young couple new in the community.

"So when he was taken to the hospital by ambulance one night, the only flowers that followed came from his immediate family. He lay in a coma for weeks. Then he was back, seen leaning on the arm of a nurse, walking the shaded paths through the woods wearing a surgical mask—an affectation, most of us thought—waving at his neighbors along the way.

"One who didn't hold a grudge had a conversation with him, and passed along the news that since the coma he often couldn't think of the word he meant to say, and the word that came out in its place was *government*. He was not aware that he said it, according to the neighbor who had heard him say that he would like to put his boat in the government and do some fishing.

"And we took it up, inviting each other over for government and coffee. Children were told that when a man and woman loved each other, the government brought them a baby. At backyard cookouts, the neighborhood refrain was, 'Put another government on the grill.'

"And we wondered why 'government' was the word that he said. Couldn't the word that came into his head as easily have been grasshopper? Or galoshes? Or ghost?

"Some of us saw it this way: there was a morning we walked our properties, taking in the damage the 'government' had done in the night. We saw broken trees and downed lines, flooded gullies and drowned flowers. And as we cleared away debris, it seemed to us that even though he didn't realize what he said when he thought he was using the word that he meant, when he invoked for protection from all that was ungovernable the word that he did, the son of a bitch was right."

A sign of getting better: without getting larger, we seem to take up more room in a room.

"Where are we?" I one day asked Warren, who said, "In a little country south of Canada, and just this side of Mexico, in a state the size of this table, in a town the size of this ashtray."

I still couldn't tell if Warren liked me. Always there is

a point when you can tell, when most people can tell. It takes longer for me. And then I'm angry with them, for it being so hard to tell. And whose fault is that? I think this is another assumption I have made a life without. I am like those people who hold grudges for what someone has done to them in a dream.

Always, we are asking here, What does a thing mean? And being asked back, What do you mean? Whereas I like to say things just to say them, because they are pleasing to say, to remember and say, "There is a tiny cove on a lake in the Sierras and I sat in its sand one late summer night when the air didn't move but was clear and dry and the lake barely lapped and the only thing that moved was a passenger ferry set forth from the other side that was strung with lights like a flirty Parisian barge and made no noise but kept coming closer," a consolation then, and now.

In the library, I found these words in the margin of an old copy of *Vogue:*

> *Why, then, did you engender me?*
> *We didn't know.*
> *What didn't you know?*
> *That it would be you.*

Warren again. In approximation of Beckett.

*   *   *

A clipping from a tabloid paper: a woman in West Virginia carried her unborn baby for more than forty years. It calcified outside the uterine wall. When questioned by reporters, the woman said, "As long as the child is inside me I haven't lost it."

A friend of mine tried to get pregnant and found out she could not. I said, "The world doesn't need more babies," and she said she wasn't going to do it for the world.

The only time the word *baby* doesn't scare me is the time that it should, when it is what a man calls me.

I brave shower after shower in which the stacks of gifts divide clearly into gifts from moms and gifts from non-moms. The moms give practical items with safety as a theme: a net to keep a crawling child from slipping through the railing of a deck, a mirror that affixes to the dashboard of a car so the driver can see the infant in the car seat behind, a dozen earnest gadgets to "babyproof" a house.

Whereas I will have chosen a mobile to hang above the crib, baby animals painted on china discs—a breath sends them swinging against one another with a sound to wake a baby down the block.

Here's a good baby story; it happened in the Caribbean sea. A woman went into labor after her husband's small fishing boat sank, and the current pulled them apart. He would later be rescued and reunited with his wife, but there was no sign of him yet when the woman's life preserver was not enough to hold her above the water. She panicked, scanning the horizon where she thought she saw a squall, the water churning with storm. It moved toward her, closing in till she could make out leaping forms; it looked to her like hundreds of leaping fish. She bobbed in the waves, enduring contractions, and the school of dolphins moved into formation around her. Later she would learn that they can locate a BB with their sonar, so it was no trouble for them to detect her daughter, about to be born.

The woman screamed when a phalanx of dolphins dove and then surfaced beneath her, lifting her above the level of the sea. But as she pushed her baby out she saw that they were there to help her, and because the dolphins were there, her daughter didn't drown.

The dolphins held their position, a buoyant grid beneath her, and kept the mother and daughter safe until human help arrived. Had help not come so soon, might the nursing mother dolphin have offered her richly fatted milk to the baby?

"They were sent to me by the Holy Father," the woman would tell her husband. "He wanted our baby to live.

"The dolphins chattered like little children," the woman said. "When my baby was born, the dolphins went wild. They bobbed up and down; their smiles were so beautiful!"

In gratitude, the woman named her daughter Dolphina Maria. The dolphins slipped away through the waves, intercessors supporting humankind on the sea, allowing us to return to land cleansed of our sins. Deep inside their bodies float the few bones left from the hind legs they once had on land.

It is such a pretty story, told to me by a Cuban woman I met in a bar at the beach. She left the bar before I did; a drunken man took her place. He leaned into me and said, "I see in your dark eyes that you have suffered, and you have compassion, and *I* have suffered, and *I* have compassion, and I see in your eyes that I can *say* things to you—"

"My eyes are blue," I said.

At the beach with Karen. Seed pods, corn cobs, smashed clams, horseshoe crabs, starfish, cartilage, bird tracks, "sea snacks."

A passing thought: "Can a woman hurt you as much as a man?"

"Worse," I tell her. "They understand you better, so they can hurt you worse."

"That's what I thought," she says.

"Nothing pulls weeds faster than frustration." I walked the rows of vegetables in the garden, and without having planned it, kneeled to pull up weeds, the right way, by

the roots. It is a satisfying task—a tangible improvement, an instant fix. I fell into a kind of trance moving
along the rows, improving the lives of beets.

In the drawer of my mother's night table, under the
emptied bottles of pills, were two pages torn from a
women's magazine. One page was a kind of consumer's
guide, a chart of deadly combinations, which pill taken with
another would make you sick, or worse. Depending on your
point of view, it was cautionary or how-to. The other
page was what I quoted a moment ago, a list of suggestions
for chasing off a gloomy mood. "Spend time in your garden. Nothing pulls weeds faster than frustration."

But wait—maybe I am confusing this page with the
page I found in her night table drawer the time she tried
to quit smoking. And she *did* quit smoking, and what a
time that was. I was in the seventh grade. I would ask her
for permission to do something, and before I could get
the question out she would have snapped back the
answer—No! Years later, I heard a joke that brought this
back. I say to you, "Ask me what is the secret of comedy."
You get as far as, "What is the secret—" and I cut you off
with, "Timing."

Yes, I went through her night table drawers, her
dresser and closets, too. What simple taste she had.
Everything she wore was unadorned. A cable in a cardigan came to seem festive. Plain black pumps. Unfrilled
slips. Not drab-classic. She wore a lot of white.

You told me you had dressed the same since you were

back in college, the khaki pants and Oxford-cloth shirts. Never bohemian, certainly no beret. Cast against type. One is tempted to say you don't look like an artist, but that is like the man who introduced me to his friend and told him I was talented, and his friend said back, "She doesn't *look* talented."

Did you ever paint a portrait of a woman you didn't like? There is a portrait I saw—the one that hangs in the Tate—where I thought you must hate the woman. Hatred is a passionate involvement. It's worse not to care for a person at all. Or is this a notion I hold onto to flatter myself?

My mother picked out all my clothes. We never went shopping together. Often what she bought was too small for me, too tight, as though she thought of me as being smaller, or wished that I was.

I said to her once, "My friends all wear their mothers' clothes," and she said, "Ask me when you're older." I got older, and asked again.

I only ever wore one thing that was hers, not that you exactly wear a purse. I carried an old brown purse she had thrown away. I took it out of the trash and hid it in my closet. On weekends, I took it, empty, to department stores. I brought it home filled with tightly rolled clothes of my own choosing. "I'm going shopping with my mother," was my private joke on a Friday; I'd come to school on Monday in a stolen sweater set. If she asked where a dress had come from, I had friends my size. I wore the stolen clothes maybe two or three times, then stuffed them in the donation box at the church on the way to school.

When my mother died, I was her size. I could have worn any of her clothes at any time. Instead I packed them in shopping bags, and drove them to the Goodwill drop. Then I had only the fear of seeing derelicts wearing my mother's clothes, her ghost in neighborhoods she didn't visit, alive.

One of the counselors here asked a single loaded question. She asked me if anyone deserved that kind of loyalty. The loyalty that would require the end of my life, as well. And it was the first time I believed the claim that you can help a person more by asking the right question than by giving them the answer.

And didn't one of your paramours do the same thing? Was that the woman you painted, the one I thought you hated in the portrait in the Tate? You didn't give her a name in the title of the portrait. You gave reporters no comment when your lady friend was found. I read she left no note—that is, if it wasn't an accident. But maybe she sent *you* a note, not that it is my business.

My mother wrote her note on a page of notebook paper, from a notebook I had used to do my homework in. Her note was four lines long. She left behind directions for what to do with "the body." She insisted there be no memorial, no mention of "this death." The note was signed and dated. There was no salutation; it was a document, nothing personal. It must have been taken by the coroner or by the police. The note was eventually returned to my father. And now it belongs to me.

I have not told the staff that I am writing this letter to you. Not when they are keen to get me talking about her. Might not a counselor gently point out the irony of our letters? Mine too long, hers too short. Might not a counselor suggest that the letter I am writing to you is the letter my mother should have written to me? Letting me get to know her. Trying to win me over.

My favorite suicide note has been fairly widely reported. It was left by a fellow who jumped from the Golden Gate Bridge: "Th-th-th-that's all, folks!"

"San Francisco," my mother once said, "is the only city that demands you love it." And she did. She wanted to keep other people alive to see it. She wanted them to have her organs, transplanted. Apparently she didn't know that the pills she took would destroy them.

I wonder what makes you angry, what happens when you are. Have you ever destroyed a canvas? You are not, I have heard, or I have read, a drinker. Does it take its toll in silence? Do you get angry with yourself? Are you, like me, your own worst critic? How do you let something out into the world when it's a sure thing someone out there won't like it?

You're good, my mother seemed to say to herself, in

fact, you're *very* good. You're just not good *enough*. My mother refused to show anyone her paintings. After a while, she stopped painting at all. What was left of her gift was the argument she had with the painter who came to paint our house and was unable to mix "her" blue.

Chatty's gentleman caller was due to arrive. Back in her room, I brushed green eyeshadow on her, but she said it made her look like she ate colored babies for breakfast. I painted on the palest lip color. "I'd sooner ride a hog to Memphis," she said.

"The Hindus have a word for this," Karen said, watching the makeup lesson. "Overexcitement. They say that when your pulse races and you get flushed and anxious, the person is bad for you."

"He was *trained* to get us overexcited," Chatty said. "By keeping himself still? By holding the best part back, and suggesting it? The best actors do that."

"Three dogs are put in a room," Warren says, and the rest of us hunker down.

"An architect's dog, a doctor's dog, and an actor's dog. Each dog is given a pile of bones and told they'll be given one hour."

Chatty blots her lips as Warren continues. "The architect's dog arranges his bones into a Cape Cod saltbox house. The doctor's dog arranges his bones into separate piles by species. The actor's dog—"

"Hand me that eyebrow pencil?" Karen says.

"The actor's dog eats all his bones, fucks the other two dogs, and asks to go home early."

"He's not an actor anymore," Chatty says. "He teaches. In a university."

Suddenly I am no longer jealous of her; I wilt at the thought of the earnest exchange of information, explanations of the way things work and who invented what.

Karen tells me about *her* trip to town with Chatty. "I found a ten-dollar bill on the grounds," Karen says, "and she told me you said it's bad luck to keep found money, I should spend it right away. So we sign ourselves out and call a cab. We get the only slow cab in the history of cabs. We miss three lights in a row, and the driver says into his rear-view mirror, 'You'd better buckle your seatbelts.' And Chatty says, 'Why? If we have an accident, I'll be out of the car before you hit anyone.'

"I didn't see anything in town I wanted to buy, but Chatty insisted I spend the money," Karen says.

Karen and I have the same shopping problem. You could set me down in Paris, I would not find a thing to buy, if what I was there to buy was something for myself. To shop for yourself requires you to know yourself. I shop for myself by default, dressing in black (though the day we met for tea I had taken a chance on gray), buying only things I have bought before that fit. I can't even think about the choices posed by makeup. To try to pick a shade of foundation is to end up in a place like this. What is peach and what is pink, what is sallow and what is fair? Skin is skin, to me, though of course you would disagree. You would know what shade of lipstick a woman should wear—a blue-red or coral, a brown-red or frost. I wonder what color you would dress me in. The moment I think a thing like this I no longer need to rouge.

But send me to find a gift for someone else, I'll show you what I can do. Christmas is never a problem for me. Most years I finish my shopping in the fall and throb until December. Although there was one year I did no shopping until December, and that with my father, in a leather store in San Francisco, for a person we had never met who was going to be our host for the holidays three thousand miles away.

My mother had died in November, on the day the United States shot off a five-megaton nuclear blast underground in Amchitka, Alaska. It caused the largest earth tremor ever produced by man. It registered 7.4 on the Richter scale, and I felt the shock in our hundred-year-old house.

People had been good to us; we had seen a lot of casseroles. We had offers of a ski house in Tahoe, of a beach house in the dunes on Monterey Bay. Someone offered us a boat—a new sixty-five-foot Chris Craft—and his captain for as long as we liked.

That was the plan, Christmas on a boat cruising the

inland waterways of Florida. Then my father and I attended a lecture on American art of the postwar period. The speaker illustrated his talk with slides. Nothing, given time, is random; one of the slides was a painting of yours. Another of the slides was a painting by Arthur Brookmyer. This particular canvas hung on a wall of our living room. It was one of a series that was the artist's self-proclaimed obsession.

The lecture ended, and my father introduced himself to the speaker. They spoke about Arthur Brookmyer. The speaker confided that he was worried about the artist—he was said to be depressed following *his* wife's death.

Driving home from the lecture, my father had an idea, the kind you can only explain as the partial result of shock, the shock of my mother's death. He wanted Arthur Brookmyer to join us for the cruise, to put on boating togs and hoist a "sea breeze" with us.

"You don't know me," my father said on the telephone, "and this may be impossible. But the invitation is given in concern and passionate admiration."

The artist said he could not join us on the boat, he had to sign new prints in Europe. So he suggested we come to *his* house, he would put us up in the guest quarters.

My father and I chose a simple shirt, classically tailored in fine toast-colored suede. It looked like the kind of thing an artist could wear in the fancy Connecticut suburb where he lived.

I did not want to spend that Christmas with a

stranger, a reportedly depressed stranger who was an intellectual and aesthetic titan who would, I feared, nail me to the floor with pointy-headed lectures on modern art. I forgot to set my alarm clock for the morning we were to leave; we were the last to board the plane for New York after a race to the airport that cut through corner gas stations so as not to hit red lights.

Brookmyer owned several houses on the property. It is not so far from your house. Since he did not own the manor house itself, he referred to himself as the tenant farmer.

In his library upstairs, I found volumes of poetry, philosophy and erotic drawings, plus catalogs from his friends' shows, including several of yours. In the guest house, the bedroom ceilings were painted the uncannily beautiful color that was, according to the tubes of paint we found in his studio, "cerulean," but which we had always called Brookmyer Blue. We'd painted the ceiling of our kitchen this color, and it was comforting to find it here, as well.

We took long walks on his property, and met up with our host at lunch and dinner. My father was in his element, but I felt immeasurably awkward. Brookmyer was thoughtful and gracious, and suffered my questions with patience. If I had known that I would meet you, I would have asked additional questions. How did he feel, I wanted to know, when a person looked at his work and said that a child could do as well? He said that it meant something when an artist arrived at a single line late in a serious career. Which did he like better, I asked, painting or drawing? "Drawing is a racing yacht cutting through the ocean," he said. "Painting is the ocean itself."

My father showed him a photograph of the artist's painting where it hung in our living room. Brookmyer told him to lower it an inch. "You should look into a painting, not up at it," he said, "especially in a room where people are sitting down."

He took us to his favorite place to eat. I was just then old enough to order a real drink, and was sipping a Bloody Mary. "It's good," I said. "What would make it great?" he asked, and when I told him he signaled a waiter and asked him to bring Tabasco.

He was a kind man with whom it was hard to talk. So I listened. I followed, somewhat, his periodic sentences as they wound to their elegant ends. My visit was years too soon. I did not make the most of it. I should have pressed him about the difference between originality and creativity, about his feeling that confusion was caused by the lack of genuine feeling.

One morning he had business in town, and told us we should inspect his studio. Feel free, he said, to pull canvases out of the racks. Turned loose like that, I looked at everything he had done. It felt like meeting relatives. It was a lesson in revision and amplification, in devotion and experimentation. The irony everpresent: that my mother was the reason we were there. She was the one who, twenty years before, had directed my father, in New York on business, to the gallery that was showing Brookmyer's work.

We embarrassed him Christmas Eve. It was too much, he said.

On Christmas morning when we went to the main house before leaving for the city, there was a large sheet of heavy paper rolled and tied with red ribbon on the dining room table. It was an artist's trial proof, inscribed with Christmas wishes to us.

I was entrusted to hold it, rolled, in the front seat of the rented car. When another car cut suddenly in front of us, I struck out my arm reflexively when my father pressed the brake, and put a dent in the painting which was eased out, at no small expense, by a framer.

On a day early in the New Year, I looked through the catalogs my father kept in his basement. I found the transcript of a talk that Brookmyer had given in his youth, and entered in my diary this fragment of a quote about the importance of an artist's capacity to absorb "the shocks of reality" and to "reassert himself in the face of such shocks, as when a dog shakes off water after emerging from the sea."

I have heard that when you taught, you were considered an excellent teacher. Every so often my mother and I tried to teach ourselves something from a how-to book.

Mostly I did things *around* her, the way nurses change the sheets with the patient still in bed.

When I turned fifteen, I asked if she would teach me how to drive. My mother wore pigskin gloves to drive, even though she drove a station wagon. She told me to ask my father for lessons. We made a date for a Saturday morning. I was ready before my father woke up. After a quick breakfast, we backed *his* car down the driveway. My mother appeared in the opened front door and called to my father that she needed his help. He called back to her that we would only be an hour. She yelled that she needed him now. She had been reading a magazine when we left, and had not looked up when we said good-bye. And there she was screaming for him as though she had opened a vein.

It was hard for me to concentrate as my father showed me the H of the gear box. I was not able to coordinate the clutch, thinking what might happen when we got home. I still can't drive a car you have to shift. Automatic is what I can manage. Isn't there enough to pay attention to *outside* the car? All I want inside a car is music. When a favorite old song comes on the radio, I can never hear it past the first few notes. The song, evocative, will take me to the place and time where I first came to hear it. I'll be taken over for the length of the song, and returned when it stops, having missed it, only knowing it was there because now it *isn't* there. The same thing happens when I think about you. Although the trajectory is different—

it is not the past, a past we haven't shared, but the future I am taken to by how quickly you have left.

I would like to go for a ride with you, have you take me to stand beside a river in the dark where hundreds of lightning bugs blink this code in sequence: right here, nowhere else! Right now, never again!

A good day. The mound in the road was not cat, but tread.

A photographer sat me down in his studio and positioned umbrella lights. He was going to make a portrait. His instructions left me hopeless—I could not look at the camera as though it was my lover. The photographer changed his tack . He said, "Give me your best 'Fuck you' look." The camera, for an instant, was my mother. "Perfect!" the photographer said.

When we can't sleep, we sneak downstairs and into the chapel, take a front pew, and hope to hear the auditory ghost, the chord that sounds at night when moonlight hits the keys through the windows in the nave. I have yet to hear it, but Chatty says it started the night the actress in the thirties made her escape.

We love our lore.

I wish I was content to think of that hour—innocent hour over cups of tea—as part of my own, a story to pass along. But I am afraid it is like the sprinkling of rain that draws the roots of plants to the surface where the sun then dries them out.

What is enough? What is ever enough?

Across the road there is an apple tree.

Every so often a car will drive past, then come back around and park beneath its branches. People will get out and start to pick the apples, pausing to bite into one, a quality check. They'll hold out the fronts of their shirts, making hammocks for the apples, and pick and take until apples are spilling out the sides of their shirts, dropping as the people return to their car hunched over from the weight of them. I have seen a woman fill her pleated skirt, then lose every one of them, slipping on the fallen ones on the way back to her car, and drive off without even one in her hand.

In the chapel I write to you on the back of an Isaac Watts hymnal, "Have I been so long with you, and yet hast thou not known me?"

Late in the fall, the sunflowers that fill a corner of the former hockey field will look like brown showerheads ready to shower seeds at the turn of a handle till the gardener clears them for compost. "A cold compost" is what Warren tells me to put on my head for a headache.

I have taken to making bouquets, with an eye to successful still life. I know it is not your strong suit, but turns out it is mine. The counselors and guests have told me as much. One school of thought says a flower arrangement should feature one type of flower—a fountain of white tulips, say, or, in the bath, one fragrant tea rose in a bud vase on a commode. But I get good notices for odd combinations: lavender cosmos and purple flowering sage, bright yellow yarrow and orange day lilies, red rambling rose spiked with flowering chive. Desperate for a hobby on a college application, years ago I wrote, "Gardening." Because my mother used to make me rake the leaves! And suddenly it comes to me that my mother never cut flowers and brought them into the house. Frustration pulls weeds; it does not arrange bouquets.

In the Hostility Suite, Warren answers the phone. "Chatty?" he says, and holds out the receiver. He waits until she is beside him, reaching for it, before adding, "Phone call for Karen."

We are teasing each other.

Maybe it is the gentle weather, but I notice we can give and take it. Dinner one warm night was a barbecue outdoors. Karen wore shorts and, for the first time, a top that was tight, a stretchy sleeveless knit. Warren looked at her chest and said, "*That* was a well-kept secret."

And Karen, she's been reading her current events,

she looked at the plate of hamburgers Warren was reaching toward; she said, "I forget how, but to produce the meat for one hamburger destroys an area of rain forest the size of a kitchen."

"That's not very big," Warren said, and helped himself.

I think of Karen, saying, "I finally solved my problem of how to talk with people," and Warren coming back with, "The hand puppets worked?"

Our own wobbly tries.

We sometimes forget why we're here. And when in a flash we remember, it is a feeling like something we're not fond of that has gone away but will be coming back. A quarrelsome mate off on a business trip.

Diminution. This is often a comfort, to be satisfied with less. My grandmother told me that when I was born, she made my mother carry me straightaway up a flight of stairs. It is a superstition. You carry the infant up the stairs so the child will rise in the world.

"Are you sure?" I used to ask her, my grandmother, because it felt as though I'd been carried instead to the basement, my job to just break even, to rise to the place where the rest were pushing off. This is not a complaint, just the way it seemed to me. Whereas take a person like Chatty. At Scrabble today, she made the word *hepper*. We challenged her. She said, "That's Southern for 'assistant'—'He's mah hepper.'" She was playing with us, but Warren looked it up and found it really is a word, the name for a salmon in its second year. And Chatty got to keep her points.

I chose the F. That time I could have played the N or F?

"It is up to you," the counselor says. "And why is getting better up to you?"

"Because," I say, my answer practiced, "I am the one who cares the most." Even when I am not.

Remember last week's storm that blew up from the tropics? Karen and I walked the beach the morning after, what beach there was left to walk. We saw four people haul in a large piece of something that, out of the surf, you could see was the hull of a good-sized sailboat. A hundred yards ahead, another piece of wood was being examined by an elderly man. He showed us the splintered stern with part of the boat's name still stenciled on it in blue:—*Wood.*

Karen and I continued down the beach, guessing at the name of the ruined boat: *Driftwood? Hollywood?* Firewood now, more's the pity. Until the missing piece washed up at our feet, and all we had to do to complete the puzzle was bend down and turn it over, and—

Touch. "Touch Wood."

So it was to the objects in the world around her that the letter writer turned.

Please excuse the switch to notebook paper; I just ran out of the good stuff. And if my penmanship suffers, it is because I am not at a desk, but in a parked car, and using my knee for support.

The driver this time is polite. He has not tried to hurry me along as other of the drivers have. He brought along a book of the stripe I could hold up to the unidentified object that flies. He brought a Thermos. And has not asked me what time it is, but has only excused himself to use the facilities across the street.

It is rabbit hour, the time they come out into the open. I wish it never got any darker than this, the moment you can no longer tell that grass is green.

If you say that you think you need to stay on, the management here says, "Of course." If you tell them you feel you are ready to move on, these same people say, "That's right." I didn't tell anyone I was trying to leave—circle of well-wishers reaching to say good-bye, reaching so that arms tangle and heads knock, yourself caught in the cross-love.

I said I had to go to town to mail a letter, to get it weighed and buy the right stamps, being careful not to drop it on the ground before it is posted. That would bring bad luck. For us both.

I asked the driver, as soon as he returned, to cut around to back behind the residential homes; there's a corridor through the dunes where you can see the ocean waves and the saltwater pond, a sanctuary for birds. Terns are quarreling in a windswept, vine-hung pine. And— worthy of your brush—three egrets stop in different poses for a second, as if they were a single bird at three consecutive moments. Now they are in motion, alighting on the sand. The tide this time of year washes hundreds of tiny starfish up onto the beach. It leaves them stranded in salty constellations, a sandy galaxy within reach.

Notes

Page 26: "The need for the new love . . ." is from "Wait," by Galway Kinnell, in *Mortal Acts, Mortal Words*, Houghton Mifflin, 1980.

Page 70: "Not every clocktick needs a martyr" is from the poem "Turning to Look Back," by John Woods, from *Keeping Out of Trouble*, Indiana University Press, 1968.

Page 79 & 119–20: The gorilla who uses sign language is Koko. Incidents cited are either from the author's visit with Koko, or from documented exchanges and observations by Koko's teacher, Dr. Francine Patterson.

Page 103: The artists referred to are Alex Melamid and Vitaly Komar, whose conceptual art piece/poll was titled "The People's Art."

Page 110: "He opens a book at random and consults randomness," is from the poem "Sortilege," by Eric Pankey, from *Apocrypha*, Knopf, 1993.

Page 143: "Drawing is a racing yacht . . ." is from Robert Motherwell in "Thoughts on Drawing," reprinted in *The Collected Writings of Robert Motherwell*, edited by Stephanie Terenzio, Oxford University Press, 1992.

Page 144: ". . . to reassert himself in the face of . . ." is from Robert Motherwell in conversation with the author and in "The Place of the Spiritual in a World of Property," (later titled "The Modern Painter's World") and in *The Collected Writings of Robert Motherwell*, ibid.

Catherine Tatge's film, *Robert Motherwell and the New York School: Storming the Citadel*, for the PBS series *American Masters*, was also a valuable reference.

ABOUT THE AUTHOR

Amy Hempel is the author of *Reasons to Live* and *At the Gates of the Animal Kingdom.* Her stories are widely anthologized in the United States and abroad and have appeared in such magazines as *Harper's, Vanity Fair,* and *The Quarterly.* She teaches in the Graduate Writing Program at Bennington College and lives in New York City.

28 ~~X4~~ DAYS